COLLECTION

SHAWN KOBB

For Jennifer,
My very own femme fatale.

Chapter 1

RED AND BLUE LIGHTS THROWN from the police cruisers colored the brick walls of the alley, creating dancing figures that vanished as soon as they appeared. Two bodies lay on the ground while another kneeled over them, prodding at one with a ballpoint pen. I stepped as close as I could without putting my loafer into the large pool of blood around them.

"Looks like you've got a busy night ahead of you," I said. If I startled him, he did a good job of hiding it.

He stood and looked me over. I didn't recognize him. Every day there were new police on the streets. The demand was high. The good news was these new recruits hadn't heard of me and didn't carry the baggage the veterans did. It made life a bit easier. Honestly, their opinion of me didn't lose me any sleep, but I was just as happy to get on without the bullshit.

"You Malone or Bowman?" he asked. He had a surprising bass to his voice, but it wasn't enough to hide his youth. The little bit of yellow fuzz he had growing on his upper lip wasn't going to fool anyone either.

"Malone. You must be new." I didn't offer my hand and he didn't seem to mind. It was in bad taste to shake hands over a couple of stiffs, especially when the blood wasn't yet dry.

"Not so new to the force, but new to DC. I was in Baltimore before. Detective Thorsen."

I nodded, but wouldn't give him more than that. Baltimore was rough. We both knew it. That didn't make him anything special, though.

"I think we're both in for a long night," Thorsen said. "They're both tagged."

He crouched again and I followed suit, careful to stay out of the mess. Thorsen pulled out a small penlight and flicked it on. The right wrist of one body was already turned up, revealing a small red tattoo of an infinity symbol, about the size of my thumbnail. The tattoo caught the light and flickered with an iridescent shimmer. The guy was chipped.

"His buddy is marked as well."

I looked over at the other man's right hand and could just see the same sideways figure-eight tattoo peeking out. When Thorsen flashed his light that way, the tat grabbed the beam and reflected it. I stood back up and dusted off my knees.

Two cases in one night and one without a head. Looking over the corpse of the second body it was all I could do to not give it a quick kick in the crotch. Instead I took out a cigar and pulled my lighter from my pocket. I used the built-in punch to ready the cigar and then slowly toasted the end while thinking of my next move.

"You got some sort of guidance what to do in this situation?" Thorsen asked.

"What sort of situation is that?" My partner, Jack Bowman, had entered the alleyway alongside Sergeant Thaddeus Valentine. If Thorsen represented the new, younger breed of DC cop who had no knowledge of my history, then Valentine was a prime example of the other camp. I ignored his scowl of greeting and looked to Jack.

"We got ourselves two clients tonight, Jack."

"Not the first time." He pulled out his own flashlight and shined it over the bodies. Even from a standing height, the infinity tattoos picked up the light and bounced it back. Both men were dressed in suits. One wore something off the rack, nothing fancy, appropriate for a million different jobs in middle management. The other guy was easily wearing five grand in the finest Italian wool with custom tailoring.

The cost to be chipped was very slowly coming down in price, but it still ran in the ten-million-dollar-plus range for the basic package. The stiff in the designer threads fit Infinity's typical client demographic. The other didn't, but we'd figure out their stories soon enough. We just needed to crack open a bit of their skulls and pull the chips out. The police could have the rest. There was only one problem.

"Where's this guy's head?" Bowman asked, nudging the corpse in the expensive suit with his toe. I instinctively glanced around as though the noggin might have just rolled away postmortem.

"That's the question, isn't it?" Detective Thorsen said.

"That's just great," Bowman said.

"Look at the bright side, Rocket," Valentine said, dropping one meaty paw on my shoulder. "For once you can't make it any worse."

"I can always make things worse, Valentine. I might start by breaking a few of those fat fingers if you don't get them off me."

Valentine stepped back, but his eyes bulged out and for a second I thought he might take a swing. He regained his composure. "You just try that, *Rocket*. See how that works out for you, *Rocket*."

He kept spitting out my nickname like his words were physical blows. Whatever made him happy. The origin of the name didn't bother me anymore. It had, once, but I'd moved on. That's what I told myself, at any rate.

"I don't suppose you have any idea where this guy's head has gone?" Bowman asked. He'd been witness to enough verbal—and sometimes physical—sparring between Valentine and me to know when to move things along.

"Not yet," Thorsen said. If he had questions about Valentine's beef with me, he kept them to himself. For a kid, he was behaving like a professional. "Based on deep lacerations on the throat of the other victim, I'd say someone was looking to take two trophies and got interrupted before he could finish."

"Was the throat-slashing the cause of death?" I asked, looking over the bodies but not seeing any other obvious signs of violence.

"What do you think, genius?" Valentine said. He laughed, but no one joined in.

"I don't think so, actually," Thorsen said, cutting off Valentine's attempt to mock me. "We'll need the full coroner's report to be certain, but take a look at this."

He crouched again and shined his penlight on the chest of the decapitated victim. The jacket was navy wool with a subtle herringbone pattern. The shirt underneath was dark gray and also of obvious high craftsmanship. The man didn't wear a tie and the top button of his shirt was undone, though the large amount of blood made it tough to make out much of his neck. I followed the beam of Thorsen's light and saw it immediately: Sticky bits of congealed, black blood painted the front of the torso and it was clear the material of his shirt was shredded.

"What is that?" Bowman asked, stepping closer.

"Stab wounds?" Valentine asked.

"Needle gun," I said quietly, more to myself than to them.

Thorsen looked up at me and nodded. "That's what I'm thinking. I had a case a few years back with a similar wound pattern."

"A needle gun? You mean like a flechette pistol?" Bowman asked.

"Sure looks like it to me," Thorsen said. "Like I said, the coroner will probably be able to tell us for certain."

"What kind of wacko uses a needle gun?" Valentine asked. "I've been a cop for twenty-seven years and I've seen every sick and twisted sort of way of killing a man you can think of. You know what I haven't seen? Someone shot by a needle gun. You know why? They don't work."

"Tell that to these guys," I said. Valentine's lack of imagination, not to mention people skills, intelligence, and personal hygiene, did a lot to explain why he was only a sergeant after twenty-seven years on the force. "They do work. You just need to know how to use them."

"What makes you an expert?" Valentine said.

When it was clear I wasn't going to answer, Thorsen spoke up. "Malone's right. Flechette technology works perfectly. It's just limited in its application. For the police or military, it's pretty worthless. If there is any distance or shielding between you and the target, the gun won't do you any good. You might as well be throwing paper airplanes at them."

"But at close range against the unsuspecting?" Bowman continued Thorsen's line of thought. "You've got a near-silent weapon that leaves very little trace and no collateral damage. An assassin's weapon."

"Right," Thorsen said. "The question is, who would want to assassinate these guys?"

"Actually," Bowman said, "I think the question is, where in the hell is this guy's head? Because all I want is a cold beer and my ass on my sofa. And I don't see that happening until we get this sorted."

"I can think of one way we might find out," I said. "You bring the bag, Jack?"

I took it from him and walked around to the client still in possession of his head. I found a relatively clean piece of alleyway to set the heavy black bag. At the touch of a button, the top split and revealed an array of sleek titanium tools. The first thing I removed was a small high-power lamp that had a built-in tripod. It was time to shed a little light on the scene. I never liked going into a guy's skull blind if I could help it.

The harsh light of the lamp washed out the red and blue of the police cruisers and turned the black pool of blood into a rich crimson. It was easier to see now that the victim's face matched his clothes. He was a white guy, probably in his late fifties, with two days' worth of beard and the tomato nose of a lifelong drunk. One eye was wide open in surprise and the other partially closed. If we were lucky, he'd seen something of the killer that could help us find his buddy's head and—more importantly—the multi-million-dollar implant inside.

"Am I good to go?"

Thorsen nodded. "We've got what we need from the scene for now. If what you can get from the chip helps us find the killer, better sooner than later."

I pulled a pair of latex gloves from the bag and then a small scanner. Turning the man's head away from me I ran the scanner over the base of his skull. The device beeped once and displayed a name and serial number.

"Stanley Morris." Thorsen jotted it down in a small notepad.

I replaced the scanner and pulled out what we in the business referred to as the "can opener." It was a titanium tool about six inches long with an ergonomically contoured handle and a textured grip. At the opposite end was a circular blade with incredibly sharp saw teeth. I'd done enough of these that I knew exactly where to line up the tool. Bracing the man's head with my other hand, I pushed the blade into the back of his skull and gave it one sharp clockwise twist. A wet crack cut through the night air, like a small tree branch snapping under foot.

"I'm gonna go check on the others," Valentine said, the light spilling into the alley showing his dark features had taken on a distinctly green sheen.

"Yeah," I said with a smirk. "You do that."

As Valentine beat a hasty retreat from the alley, I retracted the perfectly circular bit of skull I had just cut from the back of Mr. Morris's head. A sticky rope of quickly coagulating blood and greasy brown hair came along for the ride. I dropped this into a clear plastic bag, sealed it, and set it on the man's chest. It would go along with the body to the medical examiner's office in case there was any helpful information in that little bit of human remains. I didn't need it to do my job.

Now that the piece of skull had been removed, a small blinking light could be seen in the base of the brain. The light alternated between electric blue and green. That was good. It meant the implant should be functioning properly. A red light would indicate a problem. A solid blue light meant the host was alive and there had better be a damned good reason you were looking at the implant. No light at all was a total failure. It had only happened twice that I knew of, and both times had involved major lawsuits and job losses.

"Blue and green," I said quietly for my partner's benefit. Jack nodded and explained the system to Detective Thorsen.

I grabbed the next piece of equipment from the bag. To the unenlightened, it might appear I was holding a pair of small BBQ tongs. Those in the business of collection would realize I was holding an incredibly sophisticated subcranial neural storage implant removal device. The design was largely based on kitchen tongs.

Clamping down on barely visible grooves about an inch from either side of the blinking LED, I thumbed the button on the handle of the tool. There was a quiet hiss as a tiny interface locked into the perimeter of the implant and functioned like a key in a lock. The light switched to solid green as it recognized the tool. After a few seconds it switched to solid blue and that was my cue to yank out the multi-million-dollar piece of biomechanical engineering. It slid out of the brain easily, leaving a slight bit of damage that would only be noticed by a trained physician.

Using the clamp, I placed the implant in the storage container Jack had taken from the bag and now held open next to me. The container was powered and would keep the implant operating at full capacity until the techs back at Infinity Corp could get to work on uploading Mr. Morris's memories for all eternity.

"And that's that," Jack said to Thorsen. "Back to the geeks for their part. We're just the repo men."

"I saw a training video a few years back when this got started, but I'd never seen it done in real life. Not nearly as disgusting as I'd expected."

I stood and brushed my pants off. Turning off the light plunged the alley into relative darkness again.

"This is actually worse than most," I told Thorsen. "Our clients are almost always big money who die at home or in some elite hospital. It isn't often we recover chips from violent deaths, apart from the odd car crash."

"Remember the plane crash?" Jack asked. "Now that was disgusting. Still got our chip back, though. Once we found the head, that is."

"Speaking of," I said. "We'll let you know what the techs get from this guy. Maybe he saw what happened. Memories right near the end of life can be a bit muddled sometimes so it may take a bit. If you get any leads on Ichabod there, please let us know."

"Definitely," Thorsen said. "Nothing about this feels right. A couple of guys getting murdered? Sure, that happens and no one ever bats an eye. One decapitated? Alright... that's getting weird."

"Killed with a needle gun?" I added. "An assassin's weapon?"

"Right," Thorsen said. "Not normal. And to top it all off, not one, but both of our dead vics have million-dollar tech implants."

"Tech that someone wanted," Jack said.

We all stood quiet for a moment. I was sure both of them were running the same scenarios I was. What was on these chips? The chip itself was valuable, but not really worth stealing for the tech alone. It was incredibly complicated and required dozens of custom machines, tools, and elaborate coding that only Infinity Corp had. No, it wasn't the technology. It was the information contained on the chip. It happened before and certainly would happen again. The question was what memories these two had.

I held out a hand to Detective Thorsen. He seemed like a good enough guy. If I was lucky, he'd stay that way, but after guys like Valentine started filling him in on my history, that was unlikely. "Someone from Infinity will be in touch once we've got Morris uploaded."

Thorsen handed a card to Jack and me. "Thanks. If anything else comes up that you think might help explain this, give me a call."

Valentine stood near the entry to the alleyway, huddled with a few other old-timers, cops just trying to avoid a bullet or a coronary for a few more years so they could start collecting pension checks. The sergeant's mouth turned up with a mocking smile as I passed. The others were all hard-eyed and accusing. Valentine was saying something as we got into the car, but I chose not to listen.

Chapter 2

ACROSS THE POTOMAC RIVER, the sterile skyscrapers of Rosslyn stood in modern contrast to the white Indiana-limestone facades of the famous monuments of Washington, DC. Of the gaudy glass-and-steel monstrosities that overshadowed our nation's capital, the headquarters for the Infinity Corporation stood tallest. It was seventy-nine stories of offices, laboratories, and secrets. A gigantic infinity symbol made of thousands of tiny LED lights crawled up and down the exterior of the building and was visible for miles. It was just a subtle display of Infinity's new wealth and power.

Ten years ago the building hadn't existed. I can't remember what stood in its place. Probably the headquarters of a bank or insurance company. Like nearly all of Infinity's nine thousand employees, I wasn't around at the beginning. I'd heard the same stories about the beginning of the company. It started with a dream and a small team of investors. It was probably all bullshit and the place screamed of secret government funding. I didn't really care as long as the checks cleared. If the rich wanted to drop twenty-five million to live on as a computer program, more power to them. To me it seemed a lot cheaper to leave a nice diary, but what did I know?

The labs and workspaces of Infinity operated around the clock. When a client died, time was of the essence. The implant was powered by the body's own natural electrical impulses. Once that was turned off, the chip only had a limited amount of internal battery. Once the juice ran out, bad things started to happen to the data collected. A small amount of corruption was expected, but too much and you ended up with some extremely pissed off family who found they've dropped a lot of non-refundable cash for a poor facsimile of a Speak & Spell with Grandpa's memories.

It was this need for speed that motivated Infinity to create the Collection Division a few years back. Jack and I were just one of four teams covering the mid-Atlantic region. Our job was to get to the client's body fast and recover the goods. It hadn't taken Infinity long to figure out that a certain type of person best fit the profile of a Collector. Former paramedics, cops, and military made up most of the ranks. Jack had been Army Corps of Engineers and I had my time on the DC police force. We knew how to work the system. If a few corners had to be cut to collect as quickly as possible, well, that's why a couple of floors of Infinity's HQ were dedicated to Legal.

Jack swiped his badge at the entrance to the underground parking and pulled up near the secure lift. It was a small group of employees actually allowed to handle the equipment and we had special privileges. The collectors and techs worked closely together and had our backgrounds checked regularly to ensure we weren't selling company secrets. I think most felt the same as I did—the pay was too good to risk it all for one big score. Not to mention I was pretty confident Infinity had ways other than Legal to deal with transgressions. Still, I'd learned to never say never. Sometimes you have to pick the long shot to make the big bucks.

I checked my watch as we rode up the elevator—just past ten. It was late enough that most of the building was quiet, with only the labs in operation. The job didn't come with regular hours, but that worked fine for me. There wasn't much in my life that was regular.

Jack also keyed us into the secure implant collection and processing section. "Your turn for paper."

"Two clients," I said as we entered the lab. "One without a head? How about a little sympathy, Jack? You take one and I'll take the other."

He gave me a flash of teeth and shook his head. "I'd love to, buddy, but that's not how it works. We've got a system. No reason to change it up just because one client is in a bit of rough shape."

"A bit of rough shape?" I was grousing, but knew if I were him I wouldn't have volunteered to take half the reporting either. It was another aspect of the job that was strikingly similar to my own days as a cop. You thought it'd be all guns and chases and badge flashing and it turned out you spent half your time filing reports. "I'll remember this the next time we get a car crash and you're up."

He held up three fingers in a scout's salute. "I promise not to complain one bit."

I dropped the bag on the workbench next to Tony Lee. He didn't look up from his computer, the giant dual monitors covered with complex code and charts that might as well have been a foreign language. Tony pushed his glasses back up his nose and then clacked a bit more on the keyboard.

Jack looked to me and smiled. We were used to it. To the collection teams, the techs back in the labs were just glorified computer support. To them, the collectors were a bunch of overpaid garbage men. Both sides liked to needle the other, and Tony's preferred approach was to ignore us for as long as possible.

I cleared my throat loudly. Tony sighed and swiveled his chair around to face us.

"I can see the bag," he said. "And I'll get to it. Just as soon as I finish this." He gave a wave at the scrolling numbers and other data currently displayed on his computer. For all I understood, it could have just been gibberish that he used to impress us.

"Special case, this one," Jack said. "It's a rush job."

The laboratory was brightly lit, all brushed chrome and color-coded wires. Tony was the only one here at the moment, but he had his own nerdy equivalents in a few other labs on the floor. Typically only one or two were on the overnight shift, but the others were on call if needed.

I could see Tony starting to huff up his narrow shoulders to complain. The collectors had to stay until the tech could confirm the implant was valid and functional. Sometimes this took a few hours. As Tony liked to remind them, compiling the data from an incredibly complex piece of machinery ripped out of a dead guy's brain was complicated. Collectors were always trying to get a rush on the verification so they could go home. Jack was notorious for it. I may have been guilty a few times myself.

"It's legit, Tony," I told him before he could complain. "We had two clients, but only one head present. The police, and more important, Infinity, need to see if this implant has any idea what happened to the other."

I saw curiosity hook him. He rarely had a chance to truly interact with an implant. Usually it was just verification that it functioned and an array of tests before moving the unit on to the guys in the Activation division.

"I'm really busy, but I'll see what I can do." He swiveled back around to his computer, and we were thus dismissed. I noticed him glance over at the bag. It was all a show and I knew he was dying to get to it, but he'd wait until we stepped away.

"I'll be at my desk doing the paper," I told him. He didn't acknowledge. "My partner here will…"

"Be going home for a beer and yesterday's pizza," Jack finished. "It's been grand."

"Don't rub it in." Only one of us needed to stick around. I'd cut out too if the shoe was on the other foot.

I was getting settled into my desk to start the paperwork while Jack checked his mail before heading out for the night. My phone rang and the display indicated it was the lobby guard. "What's he want?"

Jack looked over and saw who was calling. "Only one way to find out."

I answered and told the guard we'd be right down.

"What's that about?" Jack asked.

"He says there's a woman in lobby and she's asking for us. Has information about the two dead guys."

"She asked for us?"

"Not by name, but she knows enough to be legit."

"So why's she here talking to us and not the police?" Jack asked. Obviously I had wondered the same thing.

"Only one way to find out," I said, mimicking Jack's southern drawl. "I guess your cold pizza isn't getting any colder."

I told Tony we'd be back in a few minutes. If he heard, he didn't give any indication, but I noticed the bag I had dropped was now open. He was working on the implant.

Chapter 3

SELENE BELLE WAS TALL WITH an athletic build that made you think she had played sports in college. Her black hair was cut short and just messy enough to be stylish, but not so put together that she gave the impression of high maintenance. I could tell she was trouble the moment I saw her. I thought Jack saw it as well, but chose to ignore the fact.

She walked away from the guard at the reception desk as soon as we exited the elevator. Clearly she had gotten what she needed from him and put him out of mind. She extended her hand, first to me and then to Jack.

"My name is Selene Belle. Thank you so much for coming down to speak with me."

"Steven Malone," I said, taking her hand. Her grip was delicate with short but perfectly manicured nails painted a red so deep as to be almost black. "This is my partner, Jack Bowman." Jack held her hand a bit too long to be decent, but she didn't seem to mind. "How can we help you, Miss Belle?"

She glanced nervously over her shoulder at the night guard still sitting at his station and making no attempt to pretend he wasn't listening to the exchange. "Is there someplace we can speak in private?"

There were a few small conference rooms on the ground floor and we took her to the closest. We ignored the large table and sat on the black leather furniture in the corner. Jack and I sat together on the sofa and Selene was on the chair next to us. She smoothed out an invisible wrinkle on her skirt before speaking.

"I need help and I'm afraid you may be the only ones that can possibly assist."

"I'm sorry," I said. "How do you even know who we are? *Do* you know? I'm not sure what we can do for you."

"Not so hasty, Rocket," Jack said. "Let's hear what she has to say." He folded his hands together and faced her with a look of complete sympathy. "What can we do for you, Miss Belle? Maybe you should start from the beginning."

Jack's concern definitely had more to do with how Selene filled that tight dress than any sort of altruism, but I had to admit I was curious. The old itch of police work came to the surface and I was eager to find a way to scratch it. This was about as close as I was likely to come.

She fixed her large, dark eyes on us and after a moment—the perfect amount of time, really—they turned wet and a single perfectly formed tear streamed down her cheek. I was impressed.

She reached into her pocket, but before she could grab anything, Jack was already offering a white linen handkerchief. I didn't know he even carried one.

"I'm sorry," Selene said. "It's just… he didn't have to kill him." She started to sob quietly and dabbed at her eyes with the handkerchief.

I looked at Jack, wondering if he was as confused as I was. Jack's mind appeared less preoccupied with such concerns. He moved over to Selene's chair and sat on the edge, dropping a comforting arm over her shoulders.

"There, there," he cooed. "It's going to be alright."

"Who didn't have to kill who?" I asked, hoping to get us back on track. I was interested, but also worried she had mistaken us for something we weren't. If she needed to be talking to the police, better to get her gone and move on. I could use some female companionship just as much as Jack, but there were easier ways to find it.

She pulled herself back together and turned off the tap. "Obviously, I don't know who the killer is, but the dead man was my lover. His name is… was Dawson Tillet."

"And which dead man was Mr. Tillet?" I asked when it was clear that Jack wasn't going to follow up. "I'm afraid I still don't understand why you're talking to us and not the police."

"I saw you come out of the alley where they died. You were there helping the police."

"The double murder tonight? Your lover was one of those guys?" I thought of the men lying in the pool of blood, one short a head. The sharper-dressed man—the one sans noggin—was dressed like someone who would enjoy Selene Belle on his arm. "How do you know?"

"Dawson was supposed to meet a contact in that alley tonight. When he never came home, I went looking for him and when I saw the police, I knew. I just knew."

"And you know what happened tonight?" Jack asked and glanced over at me. I shared his look. How did one delicately ask someone if their ex was the one with or without a head?

"I know he was murdered," she said with a sharp edge to her voice. "I know that someone cut... cut off his..." She started crying again into the handkerchief while Jack gave her a little hug.

"We're really sorry for your loss, Miss Belle, but if you know something about the murder you need to be speaking with the police. Not with us."

"I can't go to the police," she said, looking up at Jack. "The man who killed Dawson called me later. He says if I don't pay him, he's going to spill everything."

"What's he going to spill?" I asked. I was suddenly nervous. If this woman was in on the murder somehow then I wanted no part in it. Pretty face or not, I wasn't going to stick my neck out for her. There were too many on the DC police force just looking for an excuse to lock me up. "If this is some sort of love triangle gone bad, you can walk right out that door."

"Come on, Rocket," Jack said. "Give her a break."

"Come on nothing. I'm not a cop anymore and you're not army. We don't go chasing murderers."

"It's not what you think," Selene cut in. "Obviously, I want justice for Dawson's death, but I'm ashamed to admit that isn't my biggest concern. I'm married. No one knew about my affair with Dawson. At least, I thought no one knew."

"So it's blackmail?" I asked. "Killing your lover just to blackmail you? Seems a bit extreme to me."

"You don't know who my husband is," she said. "And you don't know Dawson. He never would have talked and whoever the murderer is, he obviously didn't have any proof. At least, not until now."

"I still don't get it," Jack said.

Unfortunately, I did. "Your lover had an Infinity Corp memory implant. He might be dead, but almost everything he knows and experienced in life is still preserved."

Selene Belle nodded, but didn't look me in the eyes. "Yes. I don't understand why he ever agreed to that monstrous device, but that's neither here nor there."

"Ah," Jack said, catching up. "You think this is why the head was taken? The killer wants to use the implant to blackmail you. If he can get that chip booted up, Dawson, or at least what is left of him, will spill everything. That's if they can get it working."

I nodded. "And that's a big if. This isn't like turning on a radio."

"Yes," she said. "I know, but I can't take that chance. If they get to Dawson's memories, I'll be ruined. And it isn't just me. My husband isn't the sort of man that will punish just me. He'll go after my family as well. He'll do everything he can to destroy me."

"And you think we'll be able to get the head back?" I asked. "I hate to break it to you, but in a case like this it is really up to the police to do their job."

"I understand," Selene said. "But when the police do find Dawson's... head, they'll contact you first."

It was true. All police, medical, and emergency responders were carefully trained to contact Infinity Corp the moment they came across a body that had the signature tattoo on the wrist. In the early days this arrangement had been rocky, but enough lawsuits had been brought and money spread around to grease the wheels of the machine. It was extremely rare that Infinity Corp collectors weren't on the scene of a death within an hour or two. If Detective Thorsen was able to track down the missing head, he'd certainly call.

"And what is it this mysterious killer is after?" I asked. "It might be better to just pay him off."

"If it was just money, I wouldn't be worried. Money isn't the problem."

"So what is the problem?" Jack asked.

Her eyes hardened for just a moment before once again softening and glistening with tears. I'm not sure Jack noticed, but I knew what I saw.

"I'd really rather not say, but let's just say it would be a humiliation and hurt those I care about."

"If the implant is found and brought here, we have to supply it to next of kin. There's no way around it. I'm not sure what we can do for you."

"I understand sometimes the implants can be a bit corrupted, particularly if they're not recovered quickly. Is that right?"

It was not exactly common knowledge. She had done her homework. The funny thing was, her lover had only died a few hours earlier, so either she was a quick study or she had looked into Infinity tech before.

"Maybe Dawson's implant will be seriously damaged, if not unusable altogether by the time you get it." She directed it to me. Selene had obviously decided I was the one that needed selling.

"Could be," I said slowly. "How likely that is depends on a lot of factors."

"How likely would it be if I were to pay you ten thousand dollars?" She looked to Jack. "Each, of course."

Jack's eyes widened and he looked to me. It was doable. We'd both been in enough training as collectors to know what had to be done to keep the memory implants secure and ready for processing. Simply doing the opposite of that was likely to corrupt the data. Plus, she was right. The longer the implant was in this dead guy's brain, the more likely it was to be corrupted with no help from us. It sounded like easy money, cash I could definitely use to buy some breathing room from a few less reputable types that wanted words with me. I was sure Jack could use the money as well. Neither of us had any particular love for Infinity. It was a job. We knew they wouldn't hesitate to send us packing if it suited them. I owed them no loyalty.

"Let me understand this," I said. "You pay us ten grand—"

"Each," Jack said.

"Each," I said. "And when we recover the implant—*if* we recover the implant—we will let you know." I gave her a nod and with my eyes filled in the rest.

Selene saw that I understood. "That's all I'm asking. Of course, I'll give you something as a show of my good-will." She pulled out a small silver clip from her pocket. It bulged with large bills, and she peeled off a grand for each of us and handed it over. "Call me when you have it and I'll pay the rest."

Jack gave me the slightest of nods. He was on board. It seemed easy money. We weren't going to be chasing after any killer, particularly not one who packed a needle gun and had a penchant for decapitation. All we had to do was sit around and wait for a phone call from the police. No risk, high reward. The kind of bet I loved. I tried to push down all of the previous "no risk" bets that had burned me in the past.

"Alright, Miss Belle," I said. "It's a deal. You know there are no promises, though. The police may not be able to track down this guy. You better have a contingency plan in place if he follows through with his threat."

She returned Jack's hanky to him and pulled her coat tighter around her chest as she stood. "I have one, Mr. Malone. Don't worry. I have every confidence in you, though. I know you won't let me down." I shook her offered hand.

"When you have more information, you can reach me at this number." She handed me a small piece of paper.

"Please, no details over the phone, though. We'll just arrange a place to meet. I can't be too careful."

I tucked the paper into a pocket. "If that's the way you want to play it, that's fine with me." Her paranoia seemed to be getting the best of her, but I'd go along with the cloak and dagger.

"I'll walk you to your car, Miss Belle," Jack said. "I'm actually on my way out as well."

"That's very kind of you, Mr. Bowman. It would make me feel safer."

As we returned to the lobby, the guard watched us cross to the front door of the building. Just before they left, Jack turned to me and gave me a double pump of his arched eyebrows. He was clearly hoping to land a bit more than ten thousand dollars out of this arrangement. I'd be happy just to pay down debts. To each his own, I guess.

Chapter 4

THE POST-COLLECTION REPORT was every bit as exciting as I expected. It was ten pages of forms, diagrams, and exposition describing how the client had died, how I'd been notified, what actions had been taken, and every possible contingency that could result. Oddly enough, there wasn't a little box to check that said, "client's head missing."

I decided that went under "other complications." I used the extra space to give a brief rundown of what my partner and I had found in the alleyway and listed the key details—Detective Thorsen's name and his phone number, minus one digit, an overview of the murder scene, and the actions Jack and I had taken. Namely, that we had brought the implant we had managed to collect back to the lab for processing.

What I failed to report was the visit by Selene Belle and her lucrative offer. I couldn't see much downside in the deal. If Dawson Tillet's head hadn't been found in the alley near the scene of the crime, by the time it was found there was likely to be corruption to the data. Miss Belle hardly needed our help to see to that. If she was willing to pay ten grand though, who was I to explain these things to her?

I needed that cash. Being a collector paid pretty well. Any job that nobody wants usually does. Infinity screened its applicants carefully. Anyone who leaped at the chance to visit corpses and pop open their skulls probably wasn't the sort of guy you wanted on the payroll. That meant they needed to find guys like Jack and me who would, and could, do the job, but for a price.

Even with a good paycheck, bad habits are hard to break. Hell, a good paycheck just exacerbated things for an addict like myself. You'd think disgrace and getting kicked off the force would have been a wake-up call. You'd be wrong about that.

I printed out my paperwork and signed it. One copy for my file and the rest moved on through the building electronically. I didn't even know where it went. Probably Legal and the number crunchers. They'd run the statistics and figure out new tweaks to the system to make more profit for the guys on the top floor. Fine-tuning usually meant telling guys like Jack or me that one of us was perfectly capable of doing the job alone. Thanks for your service. Here's a gold watch and a plaque with your name on it.

"That's it for me, Tony," I called over to him. He didn't answer, either too engrossed in his data or simply unwilling to respond. Not one for workplace banter, that Tony.

I grabbed my jacket and threw it over my arm and stopped at his work space on my way out. Lack of social grace or not, I wanted to hear what he'd found out on the implant we brought in. It'd only been an hour, but Tony was good at his job. I wouldn't deny it. If anyone could get a chip up and running this quick, it'd be him.

"Our client telling any stories yet?" I asked, standing over his shoulder and looking at his bewildering screens. The cybernetic implant was jacked into a reader near the computer. It wasn't all that different from the USB drives of my youth.

"The data seems clean," Tony said without looking back to me. "There's not much I can do to find out what happened in the last minutes, though, without the key from Activation. I pinged them, but their after-hours guy hasn't gotten back to me yet."

It was one of the checks and balances Infinity Corp had in place to prevent unauthorized access to the client's memories. Jack and I collected, but had no way of accessing the data. Techs like Tony cleaned things up and ran the necessary verification protocols, but the juicy stuff—the actual communication with the dead—was done by the staff in Activation. Only they could access the key, a sort of password, to get to the goods. It was this key that would be passed along to the client's loved ones per his or her instructions. We had one nutty billionaire who'd left her key only to her cat. I never did hear if the feline managed to input the code.

"You know Activation. They'll get to you when they're damn good and ready."

"Suits who think just because they can run a simple half-duplex data decryption program they're the real deal," Tony said. "If I didn't do all the heavy lifting up front, all they'd have is a million-dollar paperweight. I'd like to see them do what I do."

"We all know you're the best, Tony," I said, dropping one hand on his bony shoulder. "Do me a favor and give me a call if Activation shows up and you get anything from the chip?"

He did his best to shrug off my hand with a weak toss of the shoulder. I went easy on him and let up. Normally giving Tony shit was a favorite pastime for Jack and me, but I might be needing him soon. No sense pissing in my own bed.

He grunted and I took that as acknowledgement he'd call.

"My cell's in the database. Call if you get anything. I owe something to the detective." It wasn't entirely a lie. I just wasn't going to pass anything on to the detective all too quickly. Anything to drag the processing of Tillet's chip would put the money in my pocket.

Tony waved his hand without taking his eyes off his monitor. I think it was my dismissal.

I gave the security guard a friendly wave as I left. It was a different man than the guy who'd let Selene Belle in earlier. They must have had a shift change. That was good. I wasn't in the mood to answer questions about my mysterious visitor. It was nearing midnight and all I wanted was my bed. As much as I needed to find out what Mr. Stanley Morris—our implant upstairs—knew, I wasn't looking forward to a wake-up call.

My car was parked on a street nearby. The building had an underground lot, but I never cared for those things. Too claustrophobic. My idea of driving was freedom and I didn't feel it stuck underground and boxed in with reinforced concrete. Some of the guys gave me grief, but I didn't care.

What I drove was nothing special. A sedan you wouldn't notice twice if it passed you by. You wouldn't even notice if it was following you. Old police habits die hard. It was just a car, but I kept it in good shape and it always got me to where I needed to go. Of all the things I liked to blow money on, a fancy car wasn't one of them.

This all goes to say that while I didn't have any sort of romantic attachment to my ride, I took care of it. I was loyal to it. This is why I was particularly pissed off to see four flats, two smashed-in headlights, and a windshield spider-webbed out from a few blows of premium Northern White Ash in the form of a Louisville Slugger.

If that wasn't enough to ruin my night, seeing the baseball bat in the meaty paw of Sergei Kudrov would certainly do the job. He bounced the bat off a matching paw and stared at me stupidly. Caveman dumb was his go-to expression, from my far-too-extensive experience. He had the beady little eyes of a snake that looked out through a virtual bird's nest of coarse black facial hair. He wore one of those ridiculous Russian hats with the furry earflaps as though he was still back in his native Siberia instead of the winter-lite climate of Washington, DC.

"Aw, I'm sorry. Was this your car, Rocket?" It wasn't Sergei, of course. He'd never get out such a complicated sentence.

Ladykiller Lou oozed around the back end of my car. If Sergei was a Russian bear, then Lou was a New York City street rat. All jerky movements and darting eyes, Lou's body could barely contain the energy within. Besides being all-around unpleasant, he was exhausting to talk to. The words flew from his mouth with barely a pause in between and at the end of each sentence, he'd look to his muscle, Sergei, for approval. Whether the Russian understood a fraction of what Ladykiller said was unimportant. What mattered was he'd do what he was told without question. If Ladykiller Lou told Sergei to smash something with a baseball bat, it got smashed.

"You go back and tell Attila I was about to call him," I said. I looked over the battered remains of my boring, perfect car. "You didn't have to do that."

"You're right," Lou said. "I didn't, but we did it anyway, didn't we, Serge?"

Sergei gave a grunt that could have been agreement. He continued to bounce the wooden baseball bat as though hoping another target would present itself soon. I started to feel my head was looking like a baseball and I didn't like it.

"I've got some money coming in soon. You go tell Attila I'll have all his money in a few more days."

"He's heard it before, Rocket. He's heard it from you. If he didn't like you so much, you'd look like your wreck here. I don't know why he's so soft on you."

"Just tell him I'll have his money soon," I repeated. "I've got a little now and I'll have the rest in a few days. You tell him."

"Look who's got himself a little windfall," Lou said, looking at Sergei. I was certain "windfall" wasn't in the Russian's vocabulary, but he gave a contented grunt nonetheless. Ladykiller Lou turned to me and smiled. "You give me a little token to prove your story, I'll see to it Attila hears about it."

There was no point in trying to resist. Ladykiller Lou was slime and he had Sergei at his back. Even worse, he had Attila's ear and I couldn't afford to piss the big man off any more than I already had. I was in for nearly nine grand and Belle's money was going to dig me out. I reached into my pocket and pulled out some of the bills, leaving the rest behind. No need to show all my cards.

Lou nodded my way and Sergei lumbered over and swiped at my hand, grabbing everything in it. His other hand held the bat, its thick end right at my eye level. I could read the label it was so close. Sergei held the handful of money toward Lou, who counted it out.

"Three hundred bucks?" he said, his lip peeling back. "I do believe you are holding out on me."

Sergei somehow received an unspoken command and, faster than I would have expected from someone so large, he shot his open hand out and wrapped his fingers around my throat. With his other hand he used the bat to create an armbar, pulling my elbow back and nearly wrenching my shoulder out of its socket. The pain was excruciating, but I could have fought back. I thought better of it and did my best to stay still and minimize the pain while Lou walked over and turned my pocket inside out. The rest of the cash fell out and he snatched it from the ground.

"Better, Rocket."

"I guess I forgot about that bit," I garbled, struggling to pull air in with Sergei crushing my larynx.

"I guess you did," Lou said. He nodded and Sergei released the armbar and pushed me back by the throat. While I hacked up bits of bloody phlegm, the Russian returned to Lou's side. "I'll tell Attila. You better deliver, though, Rocket. I think his patience is running thin. Next time he might not tell me to be so nice."

"I'll have his money." I rubbed my throat, trying to massage the pain away.

"See that you do," Lou said. They turned and walked toward a nearby blacked-out Escalade, one of the few vehicles big enough to fit both Sergei's bulk and Lou's ego. Without turning back I could hear Lou. "Maybe a nice walk in the night air will give you a good chance to reflect on your life choices."

Just what I needed—self-help advice from Master Blaster. I turned and started the long walk home.

Chapter 5

LADYKILLER LOU WAS AN IDIOTIC little weasel and, as best I could tell, Sergei had no brain at all in his big, furry head. Lou was right about one thing, though. The walk home did give me a chance to think things over. Unfortunately, that gave me a chance to see how shit my life had become. You win some and you lose some.

From the high-rise buildings of Rosslyn, I crossed over Key Bridge and back into the District. The once posh Georgetown of my youth was pretty low rent these days. The college kids had largely drifted away, scared off by the rising violence and the superior options for education found online. It was good news for me. I managed to rent a small place just off Wisconsin Avenue that would have cost four times as much when I was kid. Of course, my downstairs neighbor was a Thai massage parlor that did a disturbing amount of business after 10 p.m. and tended toward the noisy side.

Between my run-in with the loan sharks and the cold night air, I felt more awake than I had all day. I thought about Selene Belle's smoky eyes and even more about the wad of C-notes she'd pulled from her purse. If I had to guess, I'd say her story was at least seventy percent bullshit. She probably knew our headless victim, but a former lover? I don't know. Maybe. It seemed like a lot of trouble to go to just to hide an affair. I thought the rich did this sort of thing all the time. I made a mental note to run her name through a few databases and see if I could dig anything up.

I didn't really care what the real story was as long as she came through with the cash. I didn't need the reminder, but Sergei's fingerprints around my throat were still there to provide one. I'd known Attila a long time and although we might be friendly, I couldn't say we were friends. In his line of business, he couldn't afford to have friends, especially former cops who couldn't do a whole lot for him anymore. If I didn't come up with his money, he'd send his goons back for an encore.

I'd kill for five minutes alone with Ladykiller Lou. I'd whip his ass up and down the National Mall and sell tickets for people to sit on the steps of the Lincoln Memorial to watch. The problem was Sergei. The big golem didn't leave Lou's side and, even worse, he did whatever he was told. I'd taken a swing at him once. It felt like slamming my fist into a cinder block. The return felt pretty similar, except against my face.

No. Fighting wasn't an option. Even if I was forced to defend myself and I shot the two—something that had crossed my mind—Attila would just send someone else. There was no shortage of toughs out there looking for work. I needed to get Attila his money, and Selene Belle looked like the best bet.

As I walked down Wisconsin I noticed the usual DC after-hours crowd eyeing me. The trick was to know which to stare down and which to avoid. I'd gotten pretty good at it. Miss Than lounged in front of her parlor smoking as I fumbled with my key.

"You look tired," she said. "Maybe you come on in for a bit? Special deal just for you." She'd probably lived in the neighborhood for at least twenty years and still spoke with some put-on Asian sex doll voice. I figured she'd done it so long for the customers that she didn't even know how to stop any more.

"Not today, sweetie. It sounds nice, though. It's been a rough evening." I gave her a nod as I finally got the door open and closed it behind me.

My apartment was small, but the price was right and I kept it clean. It worked. It could have used a bit of a woman's touch, perhaps, but there was too much baggage that came along with that particular perk. I'd handle my own decorating in the meantime.

I hadn't even managed to sit down yet before my cell rang. Looking at the wall clock, I saw it was well past midnight. Whoever was calling better have a good reason. The screen was no help, with only "Unknown Caller" displayed.

"Malone."

I listened as Detective Thorsen explained where he was and what had happened. I told him my car was in the shop—or soon would be—and he agreed to send a patrol car by to pick me up in a few minutes.

I hung up and went to the bathroom to splash a bit of cold water on my face. The man in the mirror looked older than he should and his chin was smoky, with a day's worth of beard building up. I ran a quick comb through my hair in a futile attempt to tame it and grabbed an apple from the kitchen for a bit of sustenance. It didn't seem sleep would be coming anytime soon. I went downstairs to wait for my ride.

—⟋⟍—

I made small talk with Miss Than for a few minutes, breathing in her cloud of secondhand smoke, and just as I'd started to light up a cigar, my ride pulled up. I slipped my antique Ronson lighter back into my jacket pocket.

It was a marked cruiser and a young woman got out of the driver side and called over the roof.

"Malone?"

I nodded and headed over. I noticed Than's arched eyebrow, but she didn't ask any questions. In her line of work it was best to observe and keep your mouth shut. I wish more people played by those rules.

The passenger seat of the police car was largely taken up by a computer, so I got in back. It wasn't the most comforting feeling, but it wasn't exactly a new one. I tried not to think about all the disgusting shit I'd seen take place in the backseat of one of these cars during my days as a beat cop. I hoped she'd washed it out recently, but made a mental note to send my suit to the cleaners when I got home.

The officer was cute and I'm sure she took a lot of crap because of it. I'd known plenty of women on the force when I was on the team. Nine times out of ten, women were the best cops in the room. They pushed themselves harder to be seen as equal, and the smart guys on the force recognized that.

She looked too young to have heard of me. "You been on the force long?" I asked her.

She glanced back at me in the rearview mirror. All I could see were dark brown eyes. "Long enough."

"Long enough for what?" I asked.

"Long enough not to waste my breath chatting with assholes."

I guess she'd heard of me after all. I let it go and we rode in silence. When someone had made up their mind, or even worse, had someone else make it up for them, I found it wasn't worth my effort to try to alter it. Chances were whatever she'd been told was probably true anyway.

With night traffic it was a quick drive up past the National Cathedral and into the large homes of northwest Washington. The cathedral was bathed in a bright—some might say holy—light of large spots set up around the perimeter. One of the two towers was made largely of translucent glass since the suicide bombing of a few years back. The church could certainly afford to rebuild it back to its original condition, but seemed to think they were making some sort of statement this way. I did my best to avoid reading the newspaper. Every day I didn't get killed by someone else's war was a win as far as I was concerned.

Once parked, I had to wait for my driver to let me out of the car. She didn't say anything and I left her to the rest of her shift and went to find Detective Thorsen. He stood in front of a large colonial-style manor that seemed to have every light on inside.

I shook his hand as I walked up. "Thanks for calling."

"No problem," he said. "I know what it's like to have a partner. I'd want to know. The body's around back, if you want to follow me."

A small path of paving stones wound around the house. I noticed the landscaping was tasteful, but a bit behind on its upkeep. A glance through the windows as we walked showed an empty residence, with only police crime scene technicians walking around.

"The house is empty?"

"It's been on the market for about three months now. My guess is the killer knew that and used the place as a decoy. I've got the techs inside to see if there is anything we can pull. Prints, DNA, fiber."

We came around the back side of the house to find two more police crime scene investigators walking around. I was probably supposed to be wearing disposable slippers, but if no one was going to say anything then I wasn't going to offer. A light over the back door illuminated the tidy yard.

Jack Bowman lay face up in the grass, two small-caliber bullet wounds to his chest. He stared straight up into the nearly bare branches of the large maple. I felt irritated more than anything. I don't think I'd go so far as to call Jack a friend. He was my partner, but we'd only been together four months and a partner in this job wasn't the same as the days back on the force. I wasn't expecting him to take a bullet for me. I guess he might have done just that, though.

"How'd you find him?"

Detective Thorsen and I kept about ten feet back from the body. "Neighbor heard the gunshots and called it in. We're lucky the officer took the time to check the backyard or else we probably wouldn't have found him 'til morning. You can take a closer look if you want."

"I'm good, thanks."

"I'm sorry, Malone."

"Me too."

"He have a wife? Family?"

"An ex. I think some family back in the Midwest, but he didn't talk about them much. A sister, I think?"

Thorsen took a few notes in a small orange notebook he pulled from his inner jacket pocket. "If you can get any contact information for them, that'll help a lot."

I nodded. "HR should have something. What's your scenario?"

"I'm not too sure yet. Do you have any idea why he'd be here? In this part of town?"

Only one idea came to mind and that was a leggy brunette with a crazy story and a wad of cash in her pocket. I'd last seen Jack walking Selene out of Infinity and he'd looked like he was at least as interested as getting into her pants as getting her money. This was a nice part of town and she might live in the area. If so, she could have known about this house. Maybe she'd lured him here. But why? Why hire us and then knock one of us off? I didn't know, but I wanted to ask her.

"I can't think of anything. He lived in southeast. What's the story with the homeowner?"

Thorsen flipped a few pages in his little notepad. "We've got the name of the former owner, but it's a bank repo. It's been empty a few months. I can't think of any ties to the owner. More likely it was just a quiet place to do the job."

I nodded. I ran a few scenarios through my head. There was no way to check them out with police all over the scene, though. I also needed to call Selene Belle. I wanted answers. Jack and I hadn't been tight, but he didn't deserve this. Some might argue I did, but I definitely wanted to avoid the possibility. I was starting to think whatever secrets were tucked away in Dawson Tillet's brain were bigger than I knew.

Chapter 6

I LEFT JACK BOWMAN'S BODY lying on the cold grass, staring up at stars he'd never see again. Detective Thorsen promised to call once he knew anything more, but I told him to wait until morning. Jack wasn't getting any deader and I needed sleep. Thorsen arranged for another patrol car to take me home and I was relieved to see it wasn't the woman from earlier. My new chauffeur had no interest in chatting and I was fine with silence.

He dropped me off and I fumbled for my keys in the neon red light of the Thai massage parlor. Even Miss Than had closed up shop, a sure sign I was out far too late. I felt drunk, but unfortunately hadn't had a drop in nearly twenty-four hours. I knew I'd have to remedy that before falling into my waiting bed.

I finally got the door unlocked and pushed it open when a voice called out quietly. "Mr. Malone?"

It wasn't much beyond a whisper and something about it led me to believe this was about as loud as it got. It was too high-pitched to ever be considered intimidating, but something about its hushed tone implied malice. As tired as I was, it could have been the sultry voice of Marilyn Monroe in her prime and it still wouldn't have been welcome.

"You have got to be shitting me," I said, turning toward the voice.

A slender man, the top of his shaved head barely reaching to my chin, stepped out of the shadow of a nearby parked car. He wore a khaki-colored safari jacket and kept his hands in his pockets, but judging by the way his right pocket bulged out, either he was very happy to see me or he had a weapon in his hand. I hoped it was the latter.

"Whatever you're selling," I said, turning back to the door, "I'm not buying."

He took a few steps closer, moving into the light of the neon sign of Miss Than's. The red glow of the captured gas reflected off his rectangular glasses and gave the appearance of two giant, pupil-less eyes. I thought of the evil robot Maximillian from the old *Black Hole* movie by Disney. When that thing floated toward the crew with its whirling blades... it freaked me out.

"But I'm not selling anything, Mr. Malone. I'm buying. I want to hire you."

"I think you've got the wrong guy."

"I'm quite certain that I have not." He took another step closer, but I cut him off.

"You're fine right where you are. While you're at it, why don't you take your hands out of your pockets?"

He stopped moving forward, but left his hands in his jacket pockets. "Forgive me. I have you at a disadvantage." He showed some small white teeth in a manner I assumed was him attempting to smile.

"My name is Mr. China."

He had a slight accent that I couldn't quite place. Because of the breathiness of his voice, I hadn't noticed at first. Despite his name, there was nothing about him that looked Asian.

"China, eh? What is that? French?"

I thought he had a bit of a minor coughing fit at first, but decided it must have been laughter. I couldn't see past his reflective red eyes, but I was willing to bet the laugh hadn't made it that far.

"That is quite funny, Mr. Malone."

"Thanks. It's a gift. So what do your friends call you?"

"I don't have any."

"That's too bad. If you're looking to hire a friend, then I know you've got the wrong guy. If you come back tomorrow and tell Miss Than I sent you, I'm sure she'll find you a lovely friend."

"She doesn't have what I am interested in, I'm afraid."

I bit my tongue. This guy left too many opportunities, but I was tired and also pretty sure he was pointing a gun at me. Whatever China wanted, I wanted to wrap it up and move on.

"It is my understanding that you were at the scene of a homicide tonight," Mr. China said.

"You're going to need to be more specific. It's been a busy night."

"Yes, indeed. At this particular homicide there was a body sans one head."

"It'd be pretty strange if he was sans two heads." I chuckled at my own joke. I was feeling a bit punchy after the long day.

China didn't smile. "Yes. Quite."

"Anyway," I replied, "yeah. I was. What's it to you?"

Mr. China opened his mouth to speak, but was momentarily illuminated by the headlights of a passing car. I could see through to his eyes; they were large, magnified by the strong lenses in his glasses. He tried to hug the building closer, to escape back into the shadows, but the car was gone as quickly as it had appeared.

"Either the police or your employer will likely find the missing head first. When you do, I would like to purchase it."

I had so many snappy comebacks running through my head I didn't know where to start. Lucky for him, I was sick and tired of the mystery surrounding my dead client. First Selene Belle appears, then Jack Bowman gets smoked in the backyard of a ritzy repo in the northwest hills of DC. Now I had to deal with this nut job.

"Why do you want it?" I asked.

"That's none of your concern. Just know that I am willing to pay a considerable sum."

"It's all of my concern. Even should I get the implant..." I took a step closer and took advantage of my superior height to look down on him. "I assume it is the implant you want, and not the head itself? Because otherwise I don't want to be part of whatever sicko fantasies you—"

"Mr. Malone," China said, taking a step back, "I can assure you this is no joking matter. I am quite serious."

"I'm serious too," I barked, dropping the smirk. "My partner died tonight, most likely because of this dead guy's memories. Now I've got not one, but two people who want me to throw away my job, risk getting arrested, and sell them the implant. What's in this guy's head?"

"You have another buyer?" Mr. China arched his eyebrows above his red eyes. "Who is this person?"

I paused a moment and then pulled a Montecristo number two from my inner jacket pocket. I gave my torch lighter a little shake and toasted the end before finally touching the blue butane flame to the tobacco. As I gave the cigar a few strong puffs, bursts of flame lit the dark night and I once again saw Mr. China's magnified eyes. We both knew I was dragging things out in an effort to test his patience. To the little man's credit, he waited.

"Selene Belle. A friend of yours?"

He laughed his eerie quiet cough once again and his small shoulders shook under the safari jacket. "I should have figured. How much is she offering?"

"No," I said. "The question is how much are you offering?"

"Very clever, Mr. Malone." China was quiet, clearly running figures in his head. I noticed that he had relaxed a bit with whatever he had focused on me in his pocket. The gun could have been a bluff, but I didn't think so. A small guy like Mr. China in the sort of tough world he must run in can't afford to bluff. If somebody calls it, that's it for him. I was sure there was a gun in that pocket, but I didn't think he'd use it. Not now, at any rate.

"Fifty thousand dollars," he said suddenly. "That is a very fair offer. What is Selene Belle offering?"

I always considered myself a pretty cool cucumber. Mr. China wasn't the first man to point a gun at me. He wouldn't have even been the first man to shoot me. Still, even I had trouble hiding my joy at the thought of fifty grand in my pocket. That'd clear up all my debts. With a little good financial management—such as picking the right pony—I could start a brand new life away from this poor excuse I currently possessed.

"I decide if it's a good deal. I need to know what I'm getting into. Fifty grand doesn't do me much good if I'm dead. My partner sure isn't getting much out of the money Selene offered him."

"That he isn't," Mr. China said. "I assure you I had nothing to do with that, though. You should ask Selene if she can make the same promise. Let me give you a bit of free advice, Mr. Malone."

"Sure," I said, blowing a big puff of smoke into his face. He coughed lightly, but otherwise did not react. "We're long friends."

"Find the implant and give it to me. I will pay you what I promised. And forget all of this ever happened. You don't want to know any more than that. You definitely do not want to know Selene Belle."

I reached up to my cigar as though to pull it from my mouth so I could speak. With a sudden flick of my wrist I tossed it into China's face. His reflexes were quick and he brought up both hands to bat it away before he could be seriously burned. A shower of burning embers illuminated his face and I saw his eyes widen when he saw me charge. With a clawed hand, I slammed my left down onto his right wrist to keep it from going back for the gun in his pocket. With my right I delivered a solid blow to his solar plexus. The air from his lungs burst from his mouth like a balloon released before it could be tied. As he stood gasping to recover his breath, I pulled a small Beretta Storm subcompact nine millimeter from his pocket. I quickly checked the other pockets and didn't find any other weapons.

I inspected the gun and found it loaded. I kept it aimed at Mr. China while he recovered from the punch. I didn't even give him everything. If I had, I might have gone right through him. The guy was as light as a baby bird.

When he could finally speak, Mr. China spat in my direction. "What did you do that for?"

"I don't like having guns pointed at me. I also don't like being told what to do."

"So you want to go in with her? Is that it? You can't trust her, Mr. Malone. Selene Belle will betray you the moment she's done using you."

"I'm not going in with anyone. I'm in this for me. Your fifty grand sounds real nice. Problem is, I'm not feeling all that trusting toward you, either. How do I know you'll deliver?"

He stared at me, still sucking in sharp breaths, trying to find the right words to convince me. He pulled his jacket back down and adjusted the belt. I had put a bit of a dent into his ensemble with my uppercut to his gut. After a moment he reached into another pocket on his jacket. I raised the gun to remind him I had it, though I was fairly certain he was no longer armed. He reached into the pocket slowly and removed a piece of paper, carefully folded.

I took it from him and opened it, keeping his gun in my hand but not too concerned about having it aimed at the man. It was clear he wasn't a fighter, at least not when it came to a fair fight. I'd have to look over my shoulder while he was around, but he was no danger to me for now.

It was an Interpol file dated two years ago. Selene Belle stared at me from a small photograph in the upper left corner, her raven hair dyed platinum. The hard data on her was spotty. No DOB or birthplace. Even her name was just a list of associated monikers: Selene Belle, Brigitte O'Hara, Margaret Fisher. The charges aligned nicely with her shifty personal data, with fraud, conspiracy to defraud, burglary, and arson being the highlights. She was listed as a fugitive and there was a phone number to call if you had any information on her current whereabouts. I wondered what the reward might be.

"I thought you might find that interesting," Mr. China said as I read over the file.

"I never pegged her as an angel. But this doesn't answer my question. Why should I trust you? For all I know, she's got a similar rap sheet on you."

He laughed again quietly, the sound of bones scraping across one another. "You are a very difficult man, Mr.

Malone. You've got me. I don't have any proof other than my word."

Now it was my turn to laugh.

"Yes," he said. "I know that doesn't mean much to you, but it does to me. And I promise that what I want is on that memory implant. It is very valuable to me. You are not, at least not after you have helped me. Get me the implant and I'll pay and be on my way. We won't have to see each other ever again. In fact, I think we would both enjoy that."

I nodded. What I wanted to see most of all was my bed. "And the girl?"

Mr. China smiled. "She and I have a history, as you have no doubt deduced. That doesn't involve you."

I didn't owe Selene Belle anything. It was quite likely she was playing me and might even be involved with my partner's murder. I'd be damned though if I let a two-bit gun like Mr. China tell me what was my business. One thing at a time.

"No promises," I said. "How do I reach you?"

"I'm staying at The Willard. You know it?"

Of course I knew it. It was one of the few truly nice hotels left in the city. With skyrocketing crime and the government in shambles, the glory days of DC were long past. "No phone?"

Mr. China shook his head. "Not in my line of work."

I understood. Few people of importance bothered with cell phones any longer. In my childhood everyone had had one, but not any longer. Too many data breaches, user tracing, and outright spying had killed them off for most. Cybernetics were still secure, but only the richest could afford them.

"No promises," I repeated.

Mr. China once again showed a row of small white teeth. "I believe we will be in touch soon, Mr. Malone."

Unfortunately, I had the feeling he was right. I watched him start to slip back into the shadows before he stopped short and turned.

"I don't suppose I might have my gun back?"

I popped open the revolver, dumped the cartridges into my hand and tossed the gun to him. He fumbled it, but caught it before it hit the ground. China gave a little half-bow that made me want to punch him in his liver again. With that he turned and disappeared.

Chapter 7

I COULDN'T REMEMBER FINALLY CLIMBING into my bed, but when I clawed my way up out of unconsciousness I found that I was still dressed apart from my shoes, which lay in the middle of the room. My mouth tasted like I had been chewing cotton balls. It wasn't so much that I couldn't remember going to sleep that bothered me; it was the fact I wasn't still sleeping. Someone was pounding hard on my front door, each beat against the wood matched by a throb in my skull.

The clock on my nightstand read 8:07. Even on days when I hadn't spent the entire previous night visiting corpses, I didn't get up this early. My gut told me whoever was knocking wasn't about to deliver good news.

"Open up, Malone," a distinctive voice shouted from the other side of the door. It took me a second to place it, but when I did I felt my already piss-poor mood sink further.

I ran a hand through my hair and pushed it out of my eyes. Unruly strands stood out at odd angles, but I didn't feel the need to pretty myself up for this guy. I slid open the deadbolt and opened the door.

Sergeant Valentine was sweating despite the coolness of the air. The very exertion of knocking on my door seemed to have nearly done him in. God protect any unfortunate cop that had to rely on Valentine to rescue him from a tough spot. He was more likely to stroke out than step up. His police uniform was tight, but he'd undone the collar and his belt hung low beneath his sizeable gut.

Detective Thorsen stood slightly behind him and had the decency to give me a sheepish nod. Thorsen looked well rested and clean cut, though he couldn't have gotten any more sleep than I had. The resilience of youth, I thought to myself, though I'm not sure that I'd pulled that off in my younger years either.

I stepped aside and they both came in, Valentine a bulldog let off leash and Thorsen the embarrassed owner. "I would say it is nice to see you, but my mother always told me not to lie."

"That's great to hear, Malone," Valentine said, looking around my meager apartment as though hoping to find something incriminating. "Because the truth is what we're here for."

I gave Thorsen's offered hand a quick shake and went to the kitchen to start a pot of coffee. "I'm tired, Valentine. If you've got something to say, you should be quick about it."

"Rough night last night?" he asked.

I gave him a hard look. I prided myself on keeping my cool. You couldn't be a good detective without a healthy dose of patience, and despite how my career had turned out, no one ever claimed I was bad at my job. I had my limits, though, and Valentine was pushing me to them.

"Yeah, I'm afraid my partner getting knocked off really threw a wrench into my social calendar last night." I measured a few scoops of whole coffee beans and put them in the grinder.

Valentine opened his mouth to speak and I flipped on the machine, drowning him out. It was the most pleasant noise I'd heard in a while even if it did send my headache screaming. Valentine scowled, his double and then triple chin wagging at me disapprovingly. He waited until I turned off the machine and opened his mouth to speak. I flipped the grinder back on. The key to a good cup of coffee is the proper grind. I smiled at Valentine and noticed Thorsen's smirk.

"And where'd you go after you left the scene of the murder?" Valentine said the moment I turned off the grinder.

I looked to Thorsen, but he didn't say anything. "Home. You can ask your guy. He dropped me off." I flipped on the coffeepot and went to the small dining table and took a seat. "Have you got more on Jack's killer?"

Valentine started to answer, but Thorsen put a hand on his shoulder. The sergeant looked annoyed, but kept his silence. Thorsen took a seat at the other spot at the table.

"Do you know this woman?" Thorsen asked. He slid a black-and-white surveillance photo across the table. It was taken from the main lobby of Infinity Corp and showed Selene Belle standing at the reception counter. They hadn't wasted any time in tracing Jack's final steps. I would have done the same.

I answered quickly, but with a lack of interest. "Not really."

"You're saying you don't know—" Valentine started, but Detective Thorsen cut him short.

"The guard at the front desk of your employer says you and Jack Bowman both spoke with her last night. As far as we can tell, she's the last person to be seen with your partner."

"I didn't say I've never met her," I said. "You asked if I know her and I don't. She came by the office last night to talk to Jack and me about the bodies in the alley."

"What was she asking?" Thorsen asked.

"She said the headless one was a lover." I got up and went to my jacket, which lay on the back of the sofa. Inside my inner breast pocket was my little Moleskin. I flipped it open. "She said his name is Dawson Tillet."

Thorsen nodded as though this wasn't new information. I had to admit the guy was impressive. If he was the new breed of cop coming into the District, maybe things could turn around. More likely he'd get chewed up like the rest of us and spat out a mangled shell a few years down the road. I hoped I was wrong, but I doubted it. There were too many schlubs like Valentine still around, dragging any sort of quality into the murky depths like an unwanted anchor.

"What was her name?"

"She didn't give one. Seemed real private." It was clear something was going on under the surface and I wasn't about to play all my cards until I knew what the others were holding. "She just wanted to know the procedure for an implant."

"That's it?" Thorsen asked.

"I think so."

"You expect us to believe this woman," Valentine said, stepping closer, "who didn't give her name, mind you, just stopped by to ask a few questions about something she could have just gone on the website and checked?"

"Have you got something you're trying to say?"

"Yeah, Malone. I think you're full of shit. Why'd she leave with Jack?"

Thorsen held up a hand to stop Valentine from saying anything more. It was clear Thorsen wanted keep a few cards close to his vest, but Valentine was too stupid to know the drill. This is why he'd never made detective and hated me as I'd shot past him back in the day.

"Jack was done for the night. I had paperwork to do. They just happened to leave together. I don't know what happened after that."

"What happened—" Valentine said.

"Is there anything else she said that you think could help us find her? Did she leave a contact number?"

"Nah. She was pretty mysterious about the whole thing. I got the impression she wanted her affair with the client kept quiet. She's probably married. She just wanted to know what would happen next with the implant."

"And what did you tell her?" Thorsen asked.

"We told her nothing would happen until it turned up. It's a police matter."

Thorsen stared at me, but I didn't blink. He knew there was more than I was letting on, but he was willing to let it ride... for now. If more dead bodies started piling up, he might not be so generous. Of course, Valentine was ready to cart me off to jail then and there.

"This broad's the last one to be seen with your partner, and you don't want to find out more? What kind of a pathetic excuse for a man are you?" Valentine leaned over me as I sat at the table. The only way he could put himself above me was when I lowered myself. "I guess I'm not surprised, Rocket. Once a lowlife, always a lowlife."

I stood quickly and Valentine almost fell over his own feet trying to scramble out of my way. I took a quick step toward him, my right coming up for a shot to his chin, but Thorsen stood and put himself between us. He put his hands against my shoulders and pushed me back.

"You get this guy out of my apartment, Thorsen, or I won't be responsible for what happens next."

"Just cool it, Malone," Thorsen said, his voice even and controlled. "It was a long night for all of us and I think we're all just tired." He looked hard at Valentine. "Isn't that right, Sergeant?"

The chunky officer planted a giant shit-eating grin on his face. "Oh yeah, I guess that must be it. No hard feelings. Right, Rocket?"

I didn't dignify his remarks with an answer. I just wanted them out. I needed to find Selene Belle. She owed me answers. Once I knew what was going on, then I'd think about working with the cops, but I wasn't about to talk until I held a good hand. I'd railroaded enough guys in my time on the force to know the game.

"Just get him out of here," I repeated to Thorsen.

The detective nodded and backed away slowly, making certain to keep Valentine headed toward the door with him. "Just do us a favor and stay in town? In case we have more questions that you can help us out with."

"Yeah," I said. "I hear you."

I closed the door behind them and rested my forehead against the cool wood. I wanted to go back to bed, but knew I couldn't. A hot shower sounded good. I needed to clear my head. This was going to be a long day and I was just getting started.

Chapter 8

IT WAS MUCH BUSIER AT Infinity Corp headquarters than it had been last night after hours. Between the hot shower and the cold, wet walk to Rosslyn, I was once again feeling alive. I could still use more sleep, but I'd get by. I wanted to see if Tony was in, or at the very least had left me any information that he had managed to recover from the implant from Stanley Morris, our other dead client. Even if it didn't point me toward the current location of Tillet's missing implant, I hoped it would at least shed some light on what I was dealing with.

Rosslyn was a city that only lived during the day. It was a mass of men and women, all wearing off-the-rack suits, moving from office building to fast food franchise to dry cleaner. I hated it, but my employer didn't consult me when they decided to set up shop here. I made a mental note to stop by the rental car stand and pick something up since Sergei had done a number on my own car. I also made a mental note to visit my heap. To add insult to injury, the city's finest had probably ticketed it since I'd left it parked overnight.

I crossed the brushed steel and glass lobby of Infinity and gave the receptionist a friendly nod. There was no sign of the security guard who had let Selene Belle in the night before. He probably worked nights and wouldn't be back until later in the day. I wanted to talk to him. My gut told me he had spoken with Thorsen and Valentine and it would help if I knew what he had said. I didn't think he could have overheard our conversation, but I didn't want to risk it.

Obviously I'd kept to myself the little bit about Selene Belle offering me and Jack ten grand each to tamper with Dawson Tillet's implant. It wasn't just my job I was worried about. They might not rat me out to Infinity—though I knew Valentine would jump at the opportunity—but I knew what they would think if they heard about this development. In my detective days I would have called that motive. If Selene was willing to offer us each ten thousand dollars, maybe I could make twenty thousand if Jack was out of the way. It was weak and I'd hardly kill someone, let alone my partner, for a stinking ten grand, but if you're looking for a break in a case, you'll grab anything.

I needed to find Selene Belle before they did. Fortunately for me, if what Mr. China had shown me was true, she wouldn't be too eager to get rolled up by a couple of cops. She'd keep her head low, but she'd pop up for me if I had something she wanted. Or at least, if she thought I had something she wanted.

I got to the labs and passed a few sympathetic co-workers who had already heard about Jack's death. People gave me looks, but so far they seemed to be of concern and not of suspicion. That was good. Before too long the police would be around asking questions and the attitude in the office would shift. The collectors weren't the most popular around the office as it was and I had never gone out of my way to make friends. My colleagues would turn on me in a minute if given a chance.

Tony wasn't in when I went by his desk. He had probably also worked late on Morris's implant and was still home in bed. I didn't have any problem with waking him up, but I thought I should see if he'd left me anything first. I left his workstation and found my own desk. I logged on to see if he'd left a message through the interoffice system.

There was a bit of junk that I quickly deleted. I scrolled through. One message from Tony to me and Jack.

The suits from Activation didn't respond to my request until 1 a.m. Of course, they weren't willing to get out of bed and come in so I cajoled the key out of them just so I could push things along. I used the words "murder" and "police investigation" as many times as possible until they caved. As you probably can guess, they gave me a one-time key designed to deactivate after use, but that one time was enough. I've never seen anything quite like the chip in this guy. It looked good on the surface, but once I entered the key and did some digging, things got real weird. The interface was real choppy, much more than I'd expect for someone brought in so soon after death. Nothing he said made any sense. It was schizophrenic. If I had to guess, I'd say the guy was sick and mentally unstable. I dug through the image files and found most of them locked down. I didn't even know that could be done. They required a different key. The only thing I got was the last image. Maybe it hadn't been locked yet since he died right afterward. I've attached it. I hope it helps. I'm getting out of here. I'm exhausted and creeped out. When I get in tomorrow I'm going to have a bit of a sit-down with the guys at Activation and find out what the hell they've been doing.

Although the techs in Tony's section hadn't invented all of the tech in the memory implant system, they were the day-to-day caretakers and felt quite possessive of it. I wasn't surprised to hear the frustration coming through

Tony's email. If Activation had been manipulating the code without letting the Verification guys in on it, there would be hell to pay.

I opened the attached image. The quality was low and mostly in black and white, with a few spots of color. The images held on the implants were always hit and miss. Generally only the strongest of impressions got saved and the quality often had to do with the emotions involved. I'd seen crystal-clear, full-color images of childhood crushes and long-dead dogs, but grainy, barely visible scenes of current spouses. It was all dependent on how strongly the client felt about the subject.

In this particular case, Stanley Morris had been killed soon after seeing this image. I could more or less make out the facial features, but I didn't recognize the man. He held his arm out and appeared to be pointing some sort of gun at our client. The body of the other man was partially obscured by Morris's own upraised hand. He must have instinctively tried to shield himself from what was coming. It would seem Mr. Morris had died facing his murderer.

Unfortunately for me, it didn't do anything to help me figure out what had happened to Dawson Tillet. I couldn't see him in the image at all. That is, unless he was the one holding the gun.

It was time to speak with Selene Belle.

When I'd first spoken to her last night—God, that seemed a long time ago now—I had thought she was more than a little bit paranoid. Now, with corpses multiplying, the police breathing down my neck, and Tony's unusual experience with Morris's memory implant, I was willing to give her the benefit of the doubt.

I left the gleaming modernity of Infinity Corp's head-quarters and walked a few blocks toward the Potomac River. There weren't many pay phones left these days, although they had gone through a bit of a resurgence as people became jaded about smartphones. I always used this particular phone to place bets. The less of a trail I could leave, the better.

A couple of homeless men had set up a camp nearby, their tent created largely from scraps of plastic, newspaper, and cardboard boxes. They were too far away—and too drunk—to hear me. I pulled a scrap of paper from my pocket. It didn't have Selene's name—or Margaret or Brigitte or whatever her true name was—written on it. Just a long series of numbers. I fed the phone a dollar and dialed.

It rang once before a husky voice answered. "Yes?"

"You know who this is?" I said, thinking her idea of secrecy wasn't an altogether bad one. "We met last night."

"Yes, of course. You have some news?"

"Maybe. Where can we meet?"

"The bar in the Willard Hotel. You know it?"

I laughed. "Yeah, I know it."

"What is it? Have I said something funny?" She sounded annoyed, like I wasn't taking her game seriously.

"No, nothing funny." I looked to my watch. "Thirty minutes?"

"I will see you there." A subtle beep and then silence on the other end of the line. I returned the receiver to the cradle.

So Selene Belle just happened to want to meet in the lobby bar of the same hotel Mr. China was staying at? The same man who clearly had an agenda against her? I didn't believe in coincidence. The two might not be working together, but clearly at least one was watching the other. Time would tell who was playing whom. For all I knew, they were both playing me. Between the two of them, they'd promised me sixty thousand dollars… seventy if I got Jack's share as well. The money was good, but I wasn't about to be a patsy in whatever scheme was going on.

Chapter 9

THE WILLARD HOTEL SAT JUST a few blocks from the White House and because of this fortuitous geography had seen its share of history. It was a grand old building and a frequent haunt of those looking to influence the powerful and those looking to be influenced. Sometimes that was oil and gun lobbyists looking to secure votes from less scrupulous members of our government and other times it was our esteemed elected officials looking to make a few extra bucks by selling votes.

The Round Robin Bar in the Willard was very much a relic of the past. The bar was small, decorated in wood, and the walls were lined with the portraits of the famous tipplers of the past. If you enjoyed sipping overpriced scotch while Mark Twain and Walt Whitman stared down on you, it was your place. Scotch was certainly my drink, but I was perfectly content to grab a bottle from the liquor store and drink at home alone like any reasonable person.

It was a bit strange Selene wanted to meet me here. The bar at the Willard was very much a "see and be seen" type of establishment. For more clandestine dealings, I could think of dozens of locations more suited to the task. I wondered if she was nervous to be alone with me. Maybe she was right to feel that way.

Before stepping into the hotel, I adjusted my tie and did my best to smooth a few wrinkles from my jacket. I didn't care what any of the stuffed shirts in the hotel thought of me on a personal level, but I have always found putting on the right air can open a few extra doors. The bar was at the back and I made my way through the light crowd waiting in the lobby to check in to the hotel.

Selene Belle sat at a small booth near the windows looking out over the street. She wore a black dress that hugged her figure at the top and swirled out just enough near the bottom to be playful rather than formal. She saw me enter and gave me a little wave of her fingers as though I wouldn't remember what she looked like after twelve hours.

Although she had coffee, I ordered sixteen-year-old Macallan neat. It'd cost a pretty penny, but this was a business meeting. Selene could pay. We didn't say anything beyond pleasantries until my whisky made it to the table. If she was nervous or anxious, she did a good job of hiding it. Selene Belle was slick. I had to give her that. I wondered again, for the hundredth time since seeing Jack's lifeless eyes staring up into the heavens, if she was behind his murder.

"Do you have it?" Her voice was barely above a whisper. "Have the police found my... Dawson's head?"

I sipped the whisky slowly and kept my eyes on hers. I'd make her sweat a bit and see if anything shook loose.

"Not yet," I said, slowly. "I've got some good leads, though."

Her lips, painted a deep burgundy, pursed ever so slightly. She relaxed almost instantly after doing it. I didn't know if it was intentional or she'd really mastered this cool image so well as to do it unconsciously at this point.

"Then why are we meeting, Mr. Malone? I'm afraid I can't offer you any more money."

"Things are getting complicated, Miss Belle, and it seems to me you're the only one with any answers."

"I don't believe I know what you mean." She looked around the room nervously. It was just a quick flick of the eyes, but I noticed. She might be expecting someone or maybe she already had backup in the room. I didn't want to tip my hand by looking around so I kept my gaze on her.

"My partner is dead. Let's start there. He was last seen with you."

"Mr. Bowman is dead?" She raised one perfectly manicured hand to her lips. It was the perfect reaction. Was it genuine? Maybe I'd become cynical. Maybe Mr. China's warnings had poisoned me against her. But I didn't know any more about him, and he was the one who had pointed a gun at me.

"What happened after the two of you left Infinity?" We spoke quietly and no one appeared to pay any attention. The bar seemed to be half locals and half tourists.

"Nothing at all," Selene said. "He walked me to my car. We said goodnight and I returned to the hotel."

"That's it? No night cap? Jack didn't offer you a guided tour of our nation's capital?"

A hint of red came to her cheeks. "He might have offered something to that effect, but I was hardly in the mood. My lover was just murdered and I'm likely to join him if my husband finds out. No, Mr. Malone. We parted ways and that was the last I saw him."

I thought over her story. It was the most likely course of events, but that didn't mean it was the truth. Still, what did she have to gain by killing Jack? She had just hired us. Why do that and then turn around and bump one of us off? It didn't make any sense.

"I'm very sorry for your loss, Mr. Malone," she said. "But I promise you I had nothing to do with it."

"I don't know. It all stinks like day-old fish."

"I will, of course, pay you his half as well should you honor our arrangement."

It's what I wanted to hear. Unfortunately, it was also what Sergeant Valentine was starting to sniff around. If he heard Jack's death could net me an extra ten grand, he'd throw me in a cell quicker than I could sneeze.

I reached into my jacket pocket and pulled out the image from Stanley Morris's final moments. I slid it across the table and Selene bent closer to see it.

"That's Dawson! What is this?"

"You're sure it's him?" I asked.

"Definitely. I know the quality isn't good, but it is definitely him. It's his chin. Is this from a surveillance camera? What is he doing with that gun?"

"We pulled this from the memories of the other guy in the alley. It would seem your man murdered him before getting knocked off himself. Why would he do that, Miss Belle?"

Before she could answer, a tuxedoed waiter came to check on us. Selene didn't acknowledge him, but I ordered a second whisky. My thoughts were just starting to clear up. One more wouldn't hurt.

"I don't know," she said. "I'm sure he must have had a good reason. Maybe this man was working with the person who murdered Dawson. Dawson killed Morris, but the partner got him anyway."

I had to admit, it wasn't a bad theory and I'd considered it myself. I didn't let anything on to Selene. I was here to get answers, not give them. Over the last twelve hours

I'd felt like I was playing a hand of five-card stud with only two cards. Now that I had a few more cards of my own, I wasn't ready to lay everything out on the table. Not quite yet.

"Who is your husband, Miss Belle? Business? Political? Crime?"

She glanced around the room again and this time I followed suit. I didn't see anything out of the ordinary.

"Yes, all of that." She dropped her voice even lower. "He's dangerous, Mr. Malone. It is really safer for you to know as little as possible. I wouldn't have even involved you at all if I wasn't so desperate."

I took a sip of my whisky, the brown nectar burning in just the right way. It was mellowing me out and smothering the headache from the night before. Knowing she was wanted by Interpol for fraud made it rather difficult for me to buy Selene Belle's story hook, line, and sinker, but I was having trouble helping myself. I don't know if it was the slight pout to her lip, the dark eyes, or just too many lonely nights, but I wanted her to be on the level. I wanted to believe that for the first time in a long time, I was the hero.

"Alright," I said at last, ending the silence that had enveloped both of us.

"Alright? Does that mean you believe me?"

"It means we need to figure out how to move forward. We still don't know where Dawson Tillet's head has gone and I am going to find out who killed Jack. I have a hard time imagining the two cases aren't somehow connected. The odds are too great."

"From what I hear, you've never been too good about calculating the odds." She bit her lip as soon as she said it and sat back in her seat. "What I mean is—"

"Yes," I said, my voice hard but level. "What do you mean, Miss Belle?"

I could see the wheels spinning, the brain searching for the best story. In the end she decided to go with the truth.

"Obviously, I had to do a little bit of research on you and Jack before I asked for help. I've told you how dangerous my husband is. I couldn't ask just anybody for help, Mr. Malone."

If she thought I'd let it drop at that, she hadn't dug deep enough into my past. "And what did this research tell you?"

"You were a cop," she said slowly. "A detective. And a good one, from what I gather, before..."

Her voice trailed off. I knew where the story led and I guess she did as well, at least from what she could pull from the various rags posing as journalism.

"Before I threw it all away and got busted for being on the take? Is that what you want to say?" My voice had an edge to it. Every time I thought I was done battling demons from the past, it seemed they popped up just long enough to bite me in the ass for a friendly reminder of how I'd ruined my life. I expected it from schlubs like Sergeant Valentine on the force. I didn't expect it from a beautiful woman like Selene Belle.

"I shouldn't have said anything, Mr. Malone. We all have a past that we would rather forget." She held on to my eyes. I felt it was a challenge. She knew any detective— former or not—worth his salt would have done some research. What did I know about her?

"That we do, Miss Belle." I knocked back the rest of my scotch and felt my blood pressure fall. "I should be going. I've still got a few good contacts in the police. I'll see what they've found out. I'm also going to touch base with my guy at Infinity who tapped into Stanley Morris's chip to get this image. Maybe there's more we can learn."

"I don't see what good that will do, Mr. Malone. I think it is better if you spend your time on other leads."

"If you want to run your own investigation, please be my guest..."

"No," she said quickly. "I'm sorry. I just don't know how much time I have before my husband finds out about my... indiscretion, and then I just..." She buried her face in her hands and sniffled quietly. I noticed the bartender give us a quick glance, but he went back to cleaning glassware when I caught his eye. He had probably seen too many breakups in here over the years to get involved.

I reached out an awkward hand and touched her on the arm. "Don't worry, Miss Belle. We'll find the chip. At any rate, it's been without power for more than twelve hours now. By the time it is found—if it ever is—there might not be any useable memories left."

She nodded and dabbed at her eyes with a napkin. The glisten of tears only highlighted her beauty. "I'm sorry. I just can't believe I ever did something so stupid as to get involved with Dawson. I know you will help me." She grabbed my wrist and gave it a gentle squeeze.

"Just lie low for the day," I told her, pulling my arm away. "I'll get back in touch as soon as I have more."

As I left the Round Robin Bar behind me, I looked back one last time, but Selene Belle hadn't been watching me leave. She was looking out the window, lost in her own thoughts.

Chapter 10

I HAD HOPED TO FIND Tony Lee back at his workstation at Infinity, but he wasn't there and I didn't know how to reach him. Instead, I'd try my luck with the guys in the Activation division. If they were smug to techs like Tony, they were downright contemptible to people in Collection.

There was rarely a need for Collection and Activation to interact. I was the guy that got my hands dirty. I dealt with the dead. As was so often whispered behind our backs, the guys in Collection were the "ghouls." I'm not sure who the first smartass was that came up with the childish moniker, but it had stuck.

Of course I'd heard the term before, but other than being negative I hadn't given its origin much thought. It was Jack who had filled me in on the gaps. He had gone through his Dungeons & Dragons phase while I was playing tight end for my high school football team. The way Jack explained it, ghouls were monsters that fed on the dead. I was pretty confident none of my colleagues had leanings toward cannibalism, but that hadn't stopped the media from running with the label. The way they saw it, some rich guy kicked the bucket, then we showed up and crouched over their corpse and cracked their skull open. Put that way, I guess it did lend itself to some wild tales. At any rate, the ghoul tag wasn't one my colleagues or I really appreciated. We had a job to do and we did it. There's no reason we had to be abused for it.

So if we "ghouls" were the ones getting our hands dirty with the recently departed, it was the suits in Activation who put on a pretty face for the family of the client. After Tony and his lot got the cybernetic memory implants cleaned up and running, it was Activation who unlocked them with the passkey and taught the designated recipient of the implant how to talk to their dead loved one. To me it was just a few steps above a cheap parlor trick, but if the bluebloods wanted to throw their money toward a half-hearted attempt at immortality, who was I try to tell them otherwise?

The Activation division had offices on the upper floors of Infinity Corp. They could console and educate grieving widows while enjoying a terrific view of our nation's capital. The receptionist at the front desk gave me a frosty stare after I announced I was from Collection. She was so perfectly put together that I wouldn't have been surprised she was some sort of next-gen android.

"And with whom do you wish to speak?" Her voice was clipped, perfect for answering phone calls.

"Whoever is working the case of client Stanley Morris. Tony Lee was the Verification tech. The chip came in last night."

She started typing on her computer before moving her eyes from me to the screen. After a second, she picked up the phone on her desk and said something so quietly I couldn't make it out. After returning the receiver to its cradle, she told me I could wait in the lounge area.

The sofa was soft black leather and chrome and had probably cost more than my car. It was certainly worth more than my car in its current state. I made a mental note to arrange for a tow. There wasn't much sense in getting it repaired until I paid Attila his money. He would just send Sergei and Ladykiller Lou to go another nine innings with it.

A frosted glass door opened and a young man in an expensive-looking three-piece suit walked out. An automatic smile came to his face, tinged with the slightest bit of sadness in his eyes. It was probably the same mask he wore for every client he met. Although we were ostensibly colleagues, he didn't know how to turn off his programming.

"Mr. Malone? My name is Taran Kall. I understand you have questions about a client."

"Mr. Kall," I said, shaking his offered hand. It was stronger than I would have guessed. He also filled his suit with an athletic physique, not at all like the techs in Verification. "My name is Malone. I work down in Collection."

He nodded, but I couldn't tell if it was because he was listening or because it was just the next step in his greeting process.

"How can I help you, Mr. Malone? As you are no doubt aware, we have an important separation of roles here at Infinity and there is not much about a client I can share with Collection."

"Yeah, I get that." I looked over at the receptionist. She didn't look at us, but I didn't like the extra ears. "Do you have someplace private where we can speak?"

He paused, appearing to run through the most efficient scenario to get me out of his life. He decided to start with the path of least resistance. "Of course. Mary," he called to the receptionist. "Is the small conference room available for the next five minutes?"

Good to know he was willing to offer me plenty of time.

"Yes, Mr. Kall. I'll unlock it."

I didn't see her make any motions, but a small frosted glass door near the seating area slid open and revealed a tranquil little room with comfortable chairs, a wall-mounted display, and a coffee bar. We took a seat and he looked at me, waiting for me to speak.

"I brought in a client last night, name of Morris. He was—"

"I'm sorry, Mr. Malone. I must correct you. You brought in the life memory implant of a client last night. We do not refer to it as the client."

"Right," I said, biting my tongue. This guy was all marketing and sales, but easier to play his game for now if it would get me some leads toward finding Dawson Tillet. "My partner and I brought in an implant last night. The client was murdered. I think quite possibly by another client named Dawson Tillet. I was hoping Activation might have recovered something that could lead me toward Tillet's implant."

"I am, of course, familiar with the case, but I do not see where you come in, Mr. Malone."

"Time is running out to collect the other implant. If we wait too long…"

He chuckled lightly. "Yes, obviously I know how the technology works, Mr. Malone. What I mean is, why are you asking? In a case as delicate as this one, Activation works through Legal to assist the police in their investigation. Should they find the missing… implant, Collection will be notified to collect. This is what separation of roles means."

I felt the blood coming to my cheeks and tried to will it back down.

"The police have asked me to help things along. I used to be police and—"

"Yes," Taran Kall said. "You used to be, but now you work in Collection."

"My partner was murdered last night and—"

"I saw the announcement. Let me say on behalf of Activation that we are all very sorry for the loss of your colleague."

If this stuffed suit cut me off one more time, there was a serious chance that the exquisitely serene small conference room was going to become much less peaceful. I decided to try a new tack. Perhaps we could be buddies.

"Look. Taran, was it? I'm just asking for a favor. Obviously we need to keep Legal in the loop, but if there is anything you guys have managed to get from the implant that could help us find Dawson Tillet, it is in all our best interest. Infinity wins, the police win, and Tillet's family wins because they get his memories."

He didn't speak and mulled it over. He didn't want to help me, that was clear, but something had him close. Judging by his four-thousand-dollar suit, manicure, and perfect teeth, I guessed vanity was the way to get through to him.

"I'll be straight with you, Taran," I said, trying my hardest to sound both easy-going and like the dumb ghoul he obviously took me to be. "I think whoever killed Dawson Tillet might have killed my partner. I'm just trying to get some leads to help the police. Anything I find that leads me to Tillet's implant, I'll feed to you. You guys in Activation are better equipped to handle things on that end. It's all just too complicated for a guy like me."

I was afraid I was laying the yokel routine on a bit too thick, but subtlety didn't seem to become Taran Kall. He smiled at me with his funeral director look of compassion.

"Yes," he said, with a nod and a sad smile. "I can imagine how you would want to help your partner. Of course, we are all upset about the loss of someone from Infinity. Even someone in Collection." He said it as though it wasn't offensive in the slightest.

"I really appreciate that. Do you have anything that can help me out? No one will know where I got the information. I promise you that."

Taran Kall considered my proposal. I'm not sure he was entirely buying my sudden Mr. Nice Guy routine, but my obvious deference and desperation seemed to strike a chord. He looked around the room as though someone might have slipped into the small conference room undetected. All this cloak-and-dagger jazz was much more exciting when you were faced with the real threats involved, like people smashing up your car, shooting your partner dead, and running off with a severed head that you really needed.

"Fine," he said at last. "Obviously I cannot tell you everything as it would be a tremendous violation of the trust Infinity maintains between client and company."

"Obviously," I echoed. I interpreted that as "obviously Infinity can't do anything to slow down the cash flow."

"We did provide a technician from Verification with a limited access key so that a final visual memory could be recovered."

Tony had already shared the image of Dawson Tillet apparently shooting Stanley Morris. I decided not to let that be known, though. Tony didn't need the suits from Activation coming down on him for helping me out. The image was something, but not enough to get me to the next level.

"I'll check with Tony Lee on the image. That could be really helpful. Is there anything else that you have been able to pull from the implant? Have you got him talking yet?"

Taran Kall sighed dramatically. "It isn't as simple as turning on a switch. There are a lifetime of memories on the implant, but bringing them to life for loved ones is tricky. It is often at least a week until the conversation routines are running smoothly."

"Way over my head. I just bag 'em and bring 'em." Kall's lip curled into a slight grimace, but if playing into his impression of Collection as a bunch of knuckle-draggers kept him talking, I was willing to sacrifice a bit of ego.

"Other than the final image, there is one more thing that might be able to help you and the police."

My ears perked up. "Yeah? And what is that?"

"Due to the violent nature of his death and the slight delay in collection, his final memories are a bit of a mess, I'm afraid. However, he seems to have been thinking—or saying, it is often difficult to tell—'the Hun.'"

It wasn't what I'd expected to hear. Worse, it was something I most definitely didn't want to hear. Taran Kall mistook my silence for confusion.

"As in Attila the Hun, I would gather. Though I am hardly a history buff."

"That's weird, alright. Nothing else besides that?"

"Not yet, but we're still working on him. As I said, we were a bit delayed in getting the implant." That was an obvious dig at me or at Verification, I'm not sure which. I didn't take the bait. More than ninety percent of the time the implants were collected immediately after death because the rich tended to die with a doctor present. They didn't get gunned down in a dark alley, have someone attempt to hack their head off, and then get discovered an hour later by a street rat. Given the circumstances, I think Jack and I had gotten him in as quick as possible.

"Thanks," I told him. "That at least gives me something to work with. I'll check out the image as well. If you have anything else that'll help, I'd appreciate a message."

He nodded, but I didn't feel it was likely I'd get much more from my colleague in Activation. That he had spoken this long with me qualified as a minor miracle.

"I don't know what 'the Hun' could refer to, but it was quite a strong final memory."

Unfortunately, I was afraid I might know exactly what it meant. It was time to find out. I hoped I was wrong.

Chapter 11

AFTER MY VISIT TO TARAN Kall in Activation, I returned to Tony's desk to see if he was in yet. He wasn't, but that wasn't too surprising. He probably wouldn't be in until later in the evening. I would have to come back later. Clearly Taran Kall knew more than he was sharing and, if I was lucky, Tony might have a guess what it was. At this point I was grasping at straws, hoping to find a clue other than the big one Kall had just dropped in my lap.

I tried to come up with another reason Stanley Morris would be thinking about the Hun in his final moments. Maybe he was a professor of ancient history and no one had bothered to mention it? Unlikely. Unless I was dealing with a true fluke of astronomical proportions, I knew exactly who was involved in Stanley Morris's death and it wasn't someone I was looking to visit anytime soon.

It was one of those bright winter days that somehow felt colder with the sun. I exited through the glass doors of

Infinity and decided to walk to the nearby car rental shop. The Washington DC metro area was not designed for getting around by foot and the public transportation system had been steadily deteriorating over the years. I'd spend all day waiting for a train to come and be rewarded with a crackhead's knife to my kidney to boot. No thanks. I'd get a cheap compact for a few days.

The lunchtime crowds were starting to thin, but there were still plenty of people walking around Rosslyn. Even with the steady throng of pedestrians, it wasn't hard for me to identify my shadow.

In my years as a detective I'd gotten pretty good at the game. Of course, in those days I was always the hunter and never the prey. Well, almost always. The final nail in the coffin of my career came when I was tailed by one of my fellow badges. He snapped the photos of me taking money from an embarrassingly low-level hood. Of all the people to get caught taking a bribe from, they had to see me with this guy. I'd taken bribes from much more respectable criminals. Those are the breaks. That was that and now I was digging expensive toys out of the brains of dead guys.

The point was, you didn't get good at tailing a suspect without learning how to spot someone trying to play the same game with you. This guy was an amateur. If he'd had any training, I never would have picked him up so easily. No, this shadow had learned his tradecraft by watching movies and guessing at the rest.

He was young, not much more than a kid, really, and wore a puffy parka, though it wasn't cold enough for such a coat. It didn't make sense for the temperature, but it did make it a lot easier to hide a weapon or two. He gave the appearance of being someone's muscle more than their spy. He wore a small knitted hat, black like his parka. If you were a woman you'd cross the street if you saw him coming. Everything about him signaled trouble; it was an absolutely terrible look for a would-be spy.

I didn't let on that I saw him and continued on to the car rental agency. My selection was rather limited: shitty blue compact or shitty red compact. I went with blue, picked up the keys, and went down into the garage to find my ride. As I entered the elevator, I saw my unwanted companion glance through the front window of the office with a look of panic and quickly turn out of sight. Now we would find out if I had been mistaken in my assessment of his abilities.

I found my car, took off my jacket and tossed it on the passenger seat. As easy as that I'd changed my appearance and profile just enough to throw off most tails. Then I returned to the elevator, hit the button marked "Lobby" and returned right to where I'd started from. The car rental agent asked if there was a problem and I told him I just needed a moment to run an errand before taking the car. He nodded without interest and went back to playing whatever game he had on the work computer.

I knew the garage exited around the corner and I started to walk that way, scanning the area for any signs of my new friend. It didn't take long. There was a car running near the corner and he sat inside, clearly waiting for me to drive by. He had both hands on the wheel in a proper ten and two. By the look of the kid, he couldn't have been driving all that long.

I walked behind the car and up to the passenger door. Before the kid even knew what was happening, I pulled it open and sat down next to him. His head whipped over to me and his eyes widened. I saw the barest bit of stubble on his chin and above his lip. His mouth opened and closed like a fish dying on dry land.

"If you've got something to say, I'd love to hear it."

"What are you doing in my car?" As young as he looked, he had a surprisingly deep voice. I still wasn't scared. His initial shock wearing off, I could see his features hardening, the macho persona he wore like a mask sliding back over his baby face. "Get the hell out."

"Why are you following me?" I asked. At this point I could think of a few different people who would put on a tail on me. It would help if this guy narrowed the choices.

"Last chance, buddy." He took his hands off the steering wheel and they now sat in his lap.

"You talk and then I'll think about moving along."

He moved quicker than I'd thought he could, but I'd seen it coming. He was clearly going for whatever he was packing under the heavy parka, but since he hadn't bothered to unzip the jacket, he had no chance of getting to his weapon before I got to him. I didn't even bother to go for his hands. I launched my right straight across the space between us and into his jaw. His hands came up after the fact to instinctively ward off the next blow, but I shot my left out to cup the back of his skull and slam him face-first into the steering wheel.

It was over in about two seconds and he was slumped over the wheel, just on the edge of losing consciousness. None of the passersby slowed. They either hadn't seen the fight take place in the car or were smart enough to pretend not to have noticed. I quickly unzipped the front of his jacket and saw he had a crisscross of underarm holsters, each holding a Glock. I took both and kept them trained on him. He groaned and slowly sat back in his seat, blood dripping from his nose. I was pretty sure I'd broken it.

"Let's try this again," I said. "Who sent you to follow me?"

He reared back his head and sprayed a wad of blood and spit in my direction. I kept the gun in my left hand still focused on him while reaching up with my right to wipe at my face. He started to laugh, his act of rebellion giving him a little burst of confidence.

"Why don't you go—"

Before he could finish, I shot my left hand out, pulling the barrel of the Glock back and catching him in the cheekbone with the butt of the stock. The scream he let out wouldn't have been out of place from a four-year-old girl who had slammed her finger in a door.

"You're starting to get on my bad side," I told him, raising my voice to be heard over his pathetic sob. "Who sent you?"

He paused, apparently trying to draw on whatever reserve of stubbornness he still had in him. I couldn't tell if the kid was genuinely tough or just stupid. My gut was leaning hard toward the latter. Sensing he might need a little more persuasion, I started forward with my left again, but pulled up short as he started talking.

"Mr. Arthur," he said quickly, flinching at the expected impact that didn't come. It was tough to make out what he said with the damage I'd done to his face. "I work for Thomas Arthur."

The name meant nothing to me. "What does Thomas Arthur want with me?"

The kid kept his head tilted back, but blood still ran freely from his noise. He gave a little shrug, already angry that he had spoken. It seemed a good bet this guy didn't know much. He was just hired help. I wasn't sure pushing him further would amount to much. I didn't know how Thomas Arthur treated him, but it would have to be pretty bad if he was more worried about betraying him than pissing me off. I'd already smashed his face in and had two guns pointed toward his small intestine.

"Where do I find your boss? I think he and I need to have a little chat."

The thug eyed me as hard as he could considering he was bleeding from the nose and had one rapidly swelling eye. The kid was as stubborn as a mule, but he seemed to finally acknowledge he had a losing hand in this game. I'd have to watch my back for a while. Hotheads like him don't forget quickly.

"He's got a room at the Watergate. He wants you to come by. That's why I've been following you."

"Maybe next time he'll just ask nicely, eh? It'd go a heck of a lot easier on those in his employ."

The kid grunted but didn't rise to the bait. So this Thomas Arthur wanted to talk to me. I had a pretty good idea what the topic of our conversation would be, but it didn't hurt to verify.

"What's your boss want with me?" I asked.

He shrugged, clearly already berating himself internally for giving up as much as he had. Truthfully, if the kid was just a gunslinger—and it was hard to imagine he could be anything more than that—he might not know much more. I decided I'd abused him enough. I'd have liked to pretend that he had absorbed the valuable lesson I had attempted to impart. Namely, don't fuck with someone tougher than yourself unless you're prepared to accept the consequences. Unfortunately for him, he didn't strike me as someone that learned on the first try. The next time he might not come off as well. I wondered if I would be the one teaching his next class.

"You tell your boss I'll pay him a visit later this afternoon. I've got other errands to attend to. I'll bring your guns back to you then. I'm afraid you'll just get yourself in more trouble if I leave them with you now, and you've already had a pretty rough day."

He bared some blood-smeared teeth at me. "I'll remember this."

"I hope so, kid." I opened the door and quickly exited before he could decide to take a swing at me from behind. Yeah. I had a pretty good feeling he and I would be tangling again soon.

Chapter 12

I LEFT THE KID BLEEDING in his car, most likely plotting half a dozen increasingly disturbing ways to kill me the next time we met. I knew I shouldn't have any problems from him until his boss was done with me, so I put him out of my mind. I didn't have any idea who Thomas Arthur was, but I was willing to bet what little of my reputation remained that he was after the memories in Dawson Tillet's brain. They were a hot commodity that was becoming increasingly more valuable as the minutes ticked by and the data further degraded.

I returned to my rental car and started it up. It smelled like stale cigarettes and cheap lemon air freshener, but it would get me where I needed to go and that was more than I could say for my car after Sergei's unrequested bodywork. I left Rosslyn and made my way to the George Washington Parkway and toward the southeast side of the District.

The day had started with three dead men, one of whom was my partner, a mysterious woman who was probably a grifter, an exotic foreigner, and more than likely the police thought I might be a suspect in Jack's murder. To go with that mess, I had no leads of my own. Now, after just a few hours of asking questions and digging, I had a few credible trails to sniff down. That was how detective work went. One bit of information falling into your lap could jumpstart a dying investigation.

I would talk to Thomas Arthur later, but first I wanted deal with this business about "the Hun." It wouldn't mean much to most people apart from vague memories from high school history class, but it had serious resonance with me. I desperately hoped I was off base with my hunch, but Fate was rarely that kind to me.

The Southeast Waterfront section of DC started nice enough around the baseball stadium, but quickly turned seedy. I passed laundromats, pool halls, and payday loan shops before finally reaching my destination. It didn't look much different from the other blocks in the neighborhood: young toughs drinking on door steps, eyeing me with hate, even younger girls eyeing me with a mix of hate and greed, and a gun shop masquerading as a military surplus store. I parked the car out front and knew it would be there when I returned. No one around here was stupid enough to mess with someone paying a visit to Attila.

A small chime rang when I pushed through the barred front door of the shop. Instead of finding myself inside the store itself, I entered a small cage with a second door. In Attila's line of work, it paid to have a bit of extra protection. A young woman, heavily tattooed and even more heavily pierced, stood behind a counter directly across from me. Inside the glass case I could see row upon row of knives, brass knuckles, and other personal protective items.

Stevie recognized me and buzzed me through the door. "Hey, Rocket. Long time, no see."

"I wish I could say it was good to see you here," I said, going up and giving her a quick peck on the cheek. "What happened to leaving this place behind for a fresh start at your cousin's in Atlanta?"

She shrugged, the movement making her shockingly elongated earlobe jiggle. "You know how things go. Maybe next year after I've saved up a bit more."

We both knew it was bullshit. Either she had chickened out, afraid to make such a big leap into the unknown, or Attila had simply decided she couldn't leave. My guess was a little bit of both.

The store was cramped, rows of used and new tactical clothing hanging on racks around the room. A small section in the corner had a few odd bits of camping gear, and old helmets and patches lined the neighboring wall. It was all show, of course. I'd never seen the stock change in the years I'd been coming in here. The real inventory was through the heavy steel door in the corner. That was where Attila ran his guns-and-ammo business. These days it was next to impossible to legally buy a gun. Only those who knew somebody like Attila were likely to get a piece. Unfortunately for everyone, the people who knew Attila were generally not the sort you wanted to have a gun. I thought of myself as an exception, but honestly I'd never been one for guns anyway.

"Can Attila see me?" There was no use asking if he was in. Attila was always in. I'd never met him outside of this building.

"Sure," Stevie said. She hit a button under the counter and after a moment the heavy steel door in the corner opened.

Ladykiller Lou oozed out, his hulking Russian shadow nowhere in sight, but presumably not far away. At least, not far enough away for me to share my true feelings with Lou before having my teeth returned to me in a small box.

"Rocket! How great to see you. It seems like you never come and visit anymore." He slipped past me and looked out the front door. "Where's that fine car of yours? Did you walk?"

"It was making a funny knocking sound so I dropped it off at the shop."

"I'm sorry to hear that, buddy. Anything we can do to help? Sergei's pretty good with his hands." He cackled and looked to Stevie, but she refused to acknowledge him. She looked at me with sad, knowing eyes. "Follow me. Attila's been real keen to talk to you."

I followed him through the steel door and into the gun room. Glass cases filled with various hand guns, silencers, extended magazines, and even a few grenades filled the small space. On one wall hung shotguns, assault rifles, and crossbows for those with an exotic touch. Opposite that wall were pieces of body armor, a riot shield, and even a few of the newest model weaponized mini-drones. What in the hell someone needed this kind of firepower for was beyond me. For a moment, I was glad I was no longer on the force. The police were seriously outgunned.

Ladykiller Lou rapped his knuckles on an even more formidable door across the room, its steel body reinforced with bands of heavier steel. There was no handle on this side and only a small sliding panel near the top to allow someone to check out who was on the opposite side. It slid open and I recognized Sergei's porcine eyes peering through. When he saw Lou he opened the door.

"Hey, comrade," I greeted the big Russian. As usual, he didn't respond other than to grunt. Every single time I saw him it seemed to be for the first time for all the recognition he demonstrated. He'd roughed me up so many times over the years that I was a bit hurt we weren't closer.

Sergei gave me a quick once-over to make sure I wasn't packing. Fortunately, I'd left the kid's guns in my car. I knew it was pointless to bring them in here.

At the end of the hall was a modern elevator, out of place given the dilapidated front half of the shop. I had been to Attila's inner sanctum a few times and knew that once you were past the shady facade of the army surplus store, the interior was as modern and high tech as Attila's considerable wealth could provide.

We went down two levels and walked into a comfortable living area decorated in the style of an old British hunting lodge. It was new. Last time it had been Japanese minimalism. The time before that I had found myself in French country. You had to hand it to Attila—he had taste and the money to blow to indulge it.

Attila sat in a large, overstuffed brown leather chair before a fireplace. Honest to God, I don't even remember a fireplace during his previous interior design phases. He never was one to half-ass these sorts of things. On a small table next to him was a crystal decanter of brown liquor, and a small highball glass was more than half full with the stuff. He smoked a cigar. It was expensive and probably Cuban. The exact opposite of what I normally smoked.

His back was to the elevator. It was a bit of psychological intimidation. He was so secure in his domain that he didn't need to know who was entering the room. If you were here, it was because Attila allowed you to be here.

"Steven," he said, one of the few to actually use my real first name. "Please have a seat."

Ladykiller Lou and Sergei hung back and I took a seat on the richly upholstered settee adjacent to Attila and the fire. It was pleasantly warm after the sharp winter air of Washington, DC. He looked at me through a haze of blue Cuban smoke. I thought about reaching for a cigar of my own, but held off. I was secretly hoping he would offer me one from his stash, but Attila wasn't known for his generosity.

"It's good to see you, Steven. It's been too long."

"Yeah, Attila. Lou and Sergei mentioned last night you wanted to chat."

He chuckled quietly and took a sip of his whisky. I didn't see any offer of whisky coming my way either. "Sometimes they do get a bit too enthusiastic about their work. I do apologize for that."

"I'm sure they just misunderstood your instructions. Look, Attila. I'll have your money in just a few more days. I'm working on something big."

"A sure bet, Steven?" Attila asked, a half-smile around the cigar in his teeth. "I think I've heard this one before."

"I'm not talking about gambling, Attila. This is work. Give me a week and I'll have everything I owe you."

"I didn't know there was so much money in pulling people's brains out. Maybe I should get into the racket."

"It's complicated, but just trust me, I'll have—"

"Trust you?" He pulled his cigar out of his mouth and the smile disappeared with it. "I'm not in the business of trust, Steven. I'm in the business of getting paid. I loan you the money. You pay it back. That is how this works. I'm not in the business of excuses, Steven. I've held up my part of the bargain. It is time you hold up yours."

When I was a kid, I once walked out on the edge of the frozen Potomac for a bet. It was stupid and I knew it. The ice cracked and spider-webbed with every step I took, but I wasn't about to lose the wager. I kept going even when I knew I was going in, even with my friends yelling for me to turn back. I nearly froze to death that day and it was almost a month before I could hear again out of my right ear, but it was worth it. The other kid paid up. He tried to tell me I'd lost the bet. That I'd fallen in. But I had won. The bet was to walk out on the river like an idiot, not stay dry.

I could feel the same treacherous ice under my feet now. I was very close to falling through and Attila would leave me with more than a bit of hearing loss if I wasn't careful.

"Five days, Attila. I'll have it for you in five days."

His typical mask of charm slid back on after a little sip of whisky. "What are you doing here, Steven? If you don't have my money, then why are you here?"

It was typical Attila. He answered my question with one of his own, leaving me to wonder if my new self-imposed deadline was the real deal. "I was hoping you could answer a question for me, Attila."

He laughed loudly, his pronounced middle section bouncing with the effort. "You are either the ballsiest man I know or the stupidest, Steven."

"You know I'm not the stupidest. Just ask Sergei over there." I nodded over his shoulder to the corner of the large room where Sergei and Ladykiller Lou sat in front of a small television, watching some idiotic game show.

"Sergei has uses that make up for his lack of education. You, on the other hand, have yet to prove yourself as useful to me as you were during your days with the police." He was right. Now I wasn't anything more than a source of income, and an unreliable one at that. "What is it you want to know, Steven?"

"Do you know someone by the name of Dawson Til-let?" I watched his face for any sign of recognition. If there was one, Attila did an excellent job of hiding it.

"I don't think so. Should I?"

"Maybe not. What about Stanley Morris?" This time the reaction was slight, but easy enough for me to spot after years as a detective. It was subtle, a tiny crinkling of the eyes and flare of the nostrils. He did his best to quickly hide it by bringing the cigar to his mouth. "That name mean anything to you?"

"No, Steven. Why are you asking me about these men?"

"Well, Morris is dead." I paused to see if that elicited any reaction, but none came. "He was a client of Infinity and I pulled an implant out of him last night. Turns out his last words were 'the Hun.'"

"And you thought of me?"

"I couldn't think of anyone else who went by that name. So yeah, I thought of you."

It was really the worst sort of nickname, a self-created one. Attila had been calling himself Attila the Hun for as long as I knew him and that went back more than twelve years now. I think in the early days of his rise to power he'd thought it made him so tough, like a big city mobster or a *Star Wars* villain. I always found it pretentious and pathetic, but knew when to keep my mouth shut. Enough time had passed that most didn't know he had created his own nom de plume and those who heard it simply knew to be afraid. I wondered what his real name was. Probably Lawrence.

"Maybe your dead client is just a scholar of history. After all, I'm told there was a famous Hun before myself." He smiled at his own little joke.

I knew I wouldn't get much more out of him and it was best not to push my luck. He clearly knew something about Morris, but not Tillet. That was a start. I hoped I could fill in the other blanks fast enough to recover Dawson Tillet's chip and get my cash before Sergei was sent to play T-ball with my skull.

"Could be. I thought you might have some ideas."

"I'm afraid I do not, Steven. It was nice of you to drop by, though." With that he turned his gaze back to the fire, completely absorbed with his cigar, whisky, and thoughts. I knew I was dismissed.

I stood and walked to the elevator, Lou and Sergei coming over to escort me. As the elevator door opened, Attila called out to us without looking back. "Five days, Steven. Do not let me down."

Ladykiller Lou giggled and got on the elevator with me. I ignored him and focused on my next steps. It was just what I needed: another timer that was counting down all too quickly. This one concerning my own head.

Chapter 13

I ATE MY LUNCH OUT of a paper sack while parked at Gravelly Point Park, watching the jumbo jets come in and out of Reagan National Airport. I knew I'd regret the greasy junk food later in the day, but I'd never been great about thinking of the ramifications of my actions. It was the story of my life.

Attila the Hun definitely knew more than he was letting on. That was clear. He didn't seem to know Dawson Tillet—not by name, at least—but he'd definitely reacted when I dropped Stanley Morris's name. That made sense, seeing as Activation had told me Morris's last words or thoughts had been of Attila. I didn't know for sure Tillet had killed Morris, though the recovered image made it look likely. I was positive Attila didn't kill Morris personally. He didn't leave his luxury bunker and he was smart enough to never get his hands dirty. But that didn't mean he wouldn't have Sergei, Ladykiller Lou, or one of a dozen other cronies do it for him.

Pushing Attila for more information wouldn't have gotten me anywhere. Even more important, I was starting to worry about how all these threads tied together. Selene Belle had said she would pay ten grand for Dawson Tillet's memory implant to disappear. Mr. China—I couldn't even think that guy's name without smirking—was offering fifty thousand, with the added info that if I were to turn Belle in to the police, there might be a reward. I desperately needed the cash to pay off Attila, but if he was somehow involved with Tillet's disappearing in the first place, how was this all going to work out?

It made my head hurt just thinking about it. My gut told me that Jack had gotten two slugs to the chest all because of this mess. I needed the cash, but I wasn't prepared to throw my life away for it. If it came to it, I felt confident I could figure out an arrangement with Attila for my debt. I was pretty sure, at least.

I crumpled up the empty sandwich wrapper and tossed it in the bag. The smell of the food overpowered the stale cigarette odor of the car. It wasn't much of an improvement. I got out of the car and tossed the trash into an overflowing bin nearby. There were a few other cars in the small lot, their occupants having lunch and watching the planes fly by.

I had a new puzzle piece to incorporate. Thomas Arthur. The name didn't mean anything to me, but he'd put a shadow on me and wanted me to see him at his room in the Watergate. If the last eighteen hours were a crystal ball into my future meeting with Arthur, he was going to want to hire me to find the chip in Dawson Tillet's brain. If I was lucky, he'd offer even more money. I only saw two problems with this scenario: One, I still didn't have the slightest idea how to find Dawson Tillet's missing head.

Two, I could only sell to one buyer. Selene Belle had the worst offer, but the prettiest face. Smarts would dictate that shouldn't matter, but even I succumbed to the occasional base urge.

Before going to the Watergate, I decided to pay a visit to Mr. China. If the payout was any indication, he wanted the chip even worse than Belle and that meant he must know more than he was letting on. I parked just around the corner from the Willard Hotel. I had a hunch Selene Belle was staying there as well and would rather not run into her quite yet, but if it came to that, I'd manage.

I didn't know the young man working the front desk, but I did some name-dropping to break the ice.

"Is Dax working?"

"I'm afraid he's off today, sir. Is there something I can help with?"

"I'm Detective Malone. Normally Dax is my point of contact, but hopefully you can help."

The desk attendant straightened his shoulders a bit and quickly glanced around, probably looking for a supervisor. "What can I do for you, Detective?"

Fortunately he didn't ask for identification that I no longer possessed. "You have someone staying here, last name of China."

He entered the name into his computer and looked at the screen. "Yes. He checked in two days ago. Room 718."

That was easy.

"When is he scheduled to check out?"

"Mr. China is booked with us for two more nights."

"He staying alone as far as you know?"

The desk attendant fidgeted a bit and looked again at his monitor. I was pressing for too much. I didn't think I could get much more out of him before he would find a supervisor.

"He is the only one on the reservation. Perhaps I should—"

"You've been a great help…" I looked closer at his name tag. "Doug. I'll be sure to pass on to Dax your good work."

Doug the desk attendant smiled broadly. "It is no trouble at all, Detective."

I turned toward the elevators before thinking of one last question. "Doug, what did Mr. China say his first name was?"

He turned back to his screen and frowned. "It just says 'Mister.' That's odd…"

"He's an odd guy. Thanks again."

I did a quick scan of the lobby and fortunately didn't see any sign of Selene Belle hanging around. For a moment I contemplated checking with Doug if she was staying at the hotel, but decided not to press my luck. If worse came to worst, they'd realize I had no legal right to ask about their guests and kick me out. It wouldn't be the end of the world, but it was a hassle I would rather avoid if at all possible.

As it was midafternoon, there weren't too many guests walking the halls. The cart of a cleaning woman stood outside the open door of room 718. I walked right in and found a young woman making the bed. She jumped with a start and mumbled something in a half-Spanish, half-English slur that I couldn't make out.

"I'm sorry," I said slowly, enunciating my words clearly. "I'm afraid I'm not feeling too well and would like to lie down. Can you come clean later? Maybe in a few hours?"

She was already on her way out of the room before I'd even finished speaking. In a hotel as nice as the Willard, the staff were well trained to stay out from underfoot. As easy as that, I'd taken over Mr. China's room. I had come with the idea of speaking to him face-to-face, but this would work as a stepping-off point.

He had seemed fastidious in person the night before, and his room reflected that. Though I had interrupted the cleaning of his room, it didn't seem to need it. A small black suitcase sat on the luggage rack and I found two suits hanging in the closet, one charcoal gray and the other a dark navy. Both were well made and immaculately pressed. There was no sign of the safari jacket he'd worn when I met him, so he must have been wearing it. There was also no sign of the gun I had returned to him, so I had to assume he was carrying that as well. That would be good to know when I ran into him next.

His room safe was locked and I didn't have the time nor the tools to try to get it open. In his suitcase I found more clothes and a small day planner. I pulled that out and tossed it on the bed. There was a baggage check sticker still attached to the handle of his bag. He'd flown to DC from CDG, which I recognized as Charles de Gaulle Airport in Paris. It was interesting and possibly explained his accent, but didn't tell me much other than to give me a good reason why I didn't like the guy. There was nothing else of interest in the bag as far as I could tell. I even searched the linings and seams, looking for secret hiding places. The suitcase definitely wasn't being used as a bank for my potential fifty thousand dollars. If Mr. China truly intended to honor his agreement, that meant he would need to access the cash somehow. I would need to remember that as well.

I thought about grabbing the day planner and making a hasty exit in case he decided to return, but decided against it. If he showed, well, I'd come to talk to him anyway. I flipped it open and started with this week. Unfortunately most of the diary was blank, and the smell of the fresh plastic and paper hinted that it had been recently bought.

Odd, considering it was December and he would only get a month's use out of the thing.

There was a single entry for today, and it was for an orchestral concert at the Kennedy Center at 7:30 p.m. Good to see Mr. China could maintain his cultural calendar around the need to hunt for the severed head of a recently murdered man.

"Fuckin' French," I mumbled.

Wednesday night in two days' time, there was a flight to Paris indicated. Either he was optimistic about how quickly the head of Dawson Tillet would re-appear, or he couldn't wait any longer. I wondered about the tight deadline, but with no further information, I'd have to hold that line of thought for another time. There weren't any entries further into the future, so I looked over his recent history. Apart from his flight here, shown two days earlier, there was nothing.

It seemed like a waste. A yearlong planner with only three entries, all in December. Two flights and one concert. I checked the book over closely, reading the front and back material, but found no other marks. The outside was made of a black faux leather and was embossed with the year. I put the day planner back in Mr. China's suitcase where I had found it and made a mental note to look into the concert.

After another quick sweep of the room turned up nothing of interest, I decided to move on to my meeting with Thomas Arthur at the Watergate. Hopefully it would prove more enlightening than this. I felt time ticking by far too quickly. I couldn't care less if the data in Dawson Tillet's memory implant degraded. That would still net me ten grand from Selene Belle, but it was hard to shake the feeling in my gut that there was more at play. My partner had been gunned down, and far too many others in the last day had gotten into the business of looking me up. I was suddenly high profile and I didn't like it.

—∿—

The lobby of the Willard Hotel was large enough that you could find a nook to duck into for a bit of private conversation, but not so grand a space that I could fail to see Mr. China and Selene Belle engaged in what appeared to be a rather heated conversation. I had come from the elevator when I saw them in a small alcove near the stairwell, half-concealed by a large potted plant.

Both argued in whispers and it was impossible for me to hear what was said from my vantage point. It seemed clear they knew each other. I had suspected that. After a moment, Selene slapped China across his face, his small wire-rimmed glasses knocked half off and dangling only by the earpiece. He adjusted them carefully and then raised his hand in what would certainly have been a backhand to Selene when I called out.

"That's enough, Mr. China. We must remember our manners."

Both whipped their heads around quickly in my direction, Mr. China's glasses almost falling off his head due to the new fitting Selene had provided. She took a step back from him and smoothed out her skirt. He was still flushed red from where she had smacked him, and his eyes were narrowed with hate.

"Mr. Malone," he said as I approached, his voice still the same oddly accented whisper from our meeting outside my apartment the night before. "How good to see you once again."

"Thank goodness you were here, Mr. Malone," Selene said. "I don't know what would have happened if you hadn't come by when you did."

"You probably would've taken a pop in exchange for the one you dished out." Selene bit her tongue and let it drop, understanding that I had seen everything. "I see we're all good friends so I guess the introductions can be skipped."

"Not friends, Mr. Malone," Mr. China said. "Business partners."

"*Former* business partners," Selene Belle added. "Mr. China seems to believe I owe him something, but I was explaining that he is quite mistaken."

"That was quite an explanation. If you had explained much more clearly he might have been knocked unconscious." China scowled and adjusted his glasses, but they no longer sat correctly. "What sort of business arrangement did you have?"

Selene Belle started to answer, but Mr. China quickly jumped in. "She hired me to help her with a task, but then abandoned me when something better came along. If she has promised you anything, Mr. Malone, I would heed you to remember this is her nature."

She sidled up to me and looped her arm through mine so that we both faced China. "Do not listen to his lies. It was a mutual parting and he is just upset—"

"A mutual parting? You left me stranded in Paris in the custody of the *gendarmerie*."

Selene Belle turned her lovely dark eyes my way and clutched my arm tighter. "There is much more to the story, Mr. Malone. I assure you of that."

"I'm sure there is, but at the moment I'm not really in the mood to hear it. I'm just passing through. I've got another appointment to keep. With Thomas Arthur."

I was hoping for a reaction from one or both of them and I got it. Selene released my arm and took an involuntary step back, her hand rising to her mouth. Mr. China let out the sudden squeal of a guinea pig being stepped on by an overzealous toddler. Both were looking more than a tad green around the gills.

"Thomas Arthur is here?" Mr. China asked quietly. "In Washington?"

"You can't meet with him," Selene said over him, her voice higher in pitch than its normal sultry tones. "You just can't, Mr. Malone."

"He is," I said to Mr. China and then faced Selene Belle. "And I can."

Before they could start again, I raised a hand to cut them off. "I take it you are acquainted with the man?"

They looked at each other, both waiting for the other to speak first. They had been all too quick to talk when I mentioned his name, but now neither seemed interested in enlightening me as to who he was or what he was doing having me followed by that kid.

"Don't all speak at once now," I said. "Tell me about Thomas Arthur."

Selene broke first. "I know that I haven't been completely forward about everything with you, Mr. Malone—"

"Yeah, I noticed."

"But I assure you it was for your own protection."

"You mean for *your* own protection," Mr. China cut in. He turned to me. "You know that I certainly haven't told you everything, but I can assure you my actions have been more honorable than hers."

He squinted his beady eyes at her, but flinched when she took a sudden step toward him. I stepped in between them to avoid a repeat of their earlier scuffle. I didn't have time for it and felt I wasn't getting anywhere.

"Let me get this straight," I said. "You two are arguing over who has lied to me the least? This is supposed to make me side with you?"

"I haven't lied at all," Mr. China said, his voice taking on a wounded tone. "I just haven't told you everything. Fifty thousand dollars for the implant in Dawson Tillet's head. No questions asked by you or by me."

"Fifty thousand dollars," Selene said, her voice rising sharply and attracting too much attention. She lowered her voice. "I cannot offer you that much, Mr. Malone, but I promise my need is greater than this insect's."

"Insect—!"

"Enough," I said, stepping between them once again. I was losing my patience quickly. I didn't have any kids for a reason. I didn't want to start parenting two adults. "Neither of you is answering my question. Who is Thomas Arthur?"

"If you do not already know him, then you don't want to," Mr. China said. "He is involved in several business interests, but all are best avoided."

"Organized crime?" I asked. Selene Belle avoided my gaze, but Mr. China gave a little shrug of his narrow shoulders. "Well, he's interested in me. He had me tailed. Somehow, I feel like I have a pretty good idea what it is all about."

Selene still didn't look at me and Mr. China offered only a wan smile and adjusted his glasses. It was clear these two wouldn't give me anything else willingly, and I didn't like having the conversation in the lobby of the Willard Hotel. I'd meet with Thomas Arthur myself, and if I needed more from these two, I'd come back and get it. I wouldn't be so friendly the next time.

"Alright," I said. "If we're going to play it this way, then so be it. I've got an appointment to keep and I plan on keeping it. I'll be in touch."

I turned quickly and walked to the front doors of the hotel. I could hear the soft, quick steps of someone behind me, probably Selene, but I didn't turn back. I decided to make her work for it. I stormed out the front doors and she caught up to me on the sidewalk, grabbing my arm.

"Please be careful, Mr. Malone," she said as she looked up at me. She was a liar, a fraud, and an international fugitive, but damn, she was easy on the eyes.

"I always am. I'll be in touch soon."

"Rocket..." she said and then smiled. "By the way, why do they call you 'Rocket'? Such a funny name for a grown man."

"It's a nickname I picked up on the force due to the quick acceleration of my career. Probably should have changed it to "Crash" later, but it's a tough thing to change a name."

She blushed and spoke. "Rocket, I was being honest inside. I can't afford to pay you as much as Mr. China, but I desperately need that information in Dawson to... go away."

"Understood."

"Does that mean, you'll help me instead of him? Or... Thomas Arthur?"

"It means I understand. What I'll actually do is still being worked out."

She looked like she wanted to argue or come up with a way to convince me to side with her, but I didn't give her the chance. I turned on my heel and returned to my piece-of-junk rental. The Watergate was waiting and I hoped I would find some answers. Because I knew one thing for sure—I wasn't getting the straight scoop from Selene Belle.

Chapter 14

THE WATERGATE COMPLEX SAT JUST off the Potomac River, and its ugly curves and mid-twentieth-century design were the distorted reflection of the sharp angles and neoclassical lines of the Kennedy Center next to it. Once it had been known only as "that place where some guys were arrested and it had something to do with President Nixon resigning." Now it had a new reputation as a miniature fortress within the city where the rich and powerful chose to live when in town.

The compound was walled and I parked in a small lot outside the primary gate. I'd been in the Watergate several times over the years. Once or twice when I was still a detective and more after I joined Infinity. The sort of people who had the means to stay at the Watergate were often the same ones who decided to throw down millions for a memory implant. Here, you were either made to feel like a king or completely unwelcome. I'd always fit into the second category.

Although the imposing walls and ornate iron gate were designed to be beautiful, they were more than capable of performing their primary function: keeping the outside world from intruding. There was a small visitors' building to the side of the gate and I presented myself.

"Steven Malone. I'm here to—"

"Yes, Mr. Malone," a perfectly coiffed woman with fiery red hair cut me off. "Mr. Arthur is expecting you. He is in B-101. Jason will escort you."

A young man walked up and gave a sort of half-bow. It must have been the kind of thing the money here liked—for servants to genuflect and grovel. It just made me want to push the kid down. Of course, working in a place like this, he was probably used to being treated like shit. That didn't make me feel good about my initial impulse.

"I've been here before. I can find my own way."

"I'm afraid it is Watergate policy to escort all outside guests."

I didn't bother to argue and followed Jason. He didn't feel the need to make chitchat, but I hoped to take advantage of the opportunity to gather some intelligence for my meeting.

"Jason, right?"

"Yes, sir."

"Have you worked at the Watergate long?"

"Just three weeks, sir."

"And have you met Thomas Arthur?"

Jason forced a smile, but I could tell I was pushing him into uncomfortable territory. "I can't say that I have had the pleasure of meeting Mr. Arthur, sir."

"Do you know if he is a permanent resident or here on a temporary stay?"

"I'm really not allowed to—"

"Yes," I said. "I understand. I don't want you to get into any trouble. But you see, Jason, I'm a police detective, so it really is okay."

"But I don't—"

"And Mr. Arthur isn't in any trouble. I'm just here to consult with him. Someone suggested he might have some information that could help me out on a case. Quite a gruesome one too…"

Jason looked over at me as we slowed our walk a bit. "A murder?"

I nodded. "A double murder."

"How is Mr. Arthur going to be able to help?" he asked, looking around to make sure that no one watched our conversation. "I thought he was only a banker?"

"He is, but I think he might have some information about one of our victims that can really help crack things open. In my line of work you need to pursue every possible lead, no matter how ridiculous it may appear at first glance."

We reached the B building and the door to room 101, which seemed to take up most of the first floor. Jason rang the doorbell and it was answered quickly by another Watergate employee in the same uniform as Jason.

"Mr. Malone to see Mr. Arthur," Jason announced. The other man gave a small nod and held the door for me.

"Thanks for your help, Jason."

He gave me a big smile and turned and left.

The foyer of Thomas Arthur's residence was larger than my apartment. The doorman led me quickly through and past several other rooms, all impeccably decorated, and out to a covered veranda that had views of the river, the Kennedy Center, and the skyline of Rosslyn across the way. The Infinity Corp tower was a dagger of steel and glass piercing the heavens like Icarus reaching for the sun. The young tough that had been tasked to follow me earlier stood off to the side. His face was bruised and his nose bandaged, but the blood had all been cleaned off. He fixed me with an icy stare, but otherwise did not acknowledge me. A heavyset white male of about sixty sat on a cushioned wicker chair.

The doorman announced me, and Thomas Arthur set the newspaper he had been reading down on the table in front of him and rose to greet me. "Ah, Mr. Malone. I am so glad that you could finally make it. I was starting to think you were not going to show."

His accent was English, or Scottish maybe. His clothes were expensive but casual, and he wore a large gold signet ring on his right pinky finger. He had the smile of a man who controlled everything around him. There was no fear, no concern. Thomas Arthur was a man who was used to getting what he wanted.

"How could I pass up your invitation?" I smiled over at the kid, but he stared straight ahead and said nothing.

Arthur chuckled. "Yes, Walter told me of your little encounter. I should have known that you would spot him right off. I do apologize for the clandestine observation."

"No harm done. Well, none to me at any rate. Your kid should learn to pick on people his own size in the future."

"I'm not sure you needed to give him such a painful lesson, Mr. Malone, but it does demonstrate that I've found the right man for the job." We both spoke of Walter as though he wasn't in the room. It seemed to me that Thomas Arthur was often surrounded by the sort of disposable people he could quickly put out of mind.

"I have a good feeling I know what that job might be." If the pattern held true, Thomas Arthur was about to offer big money for the chip in Dawson Tillet's head. A chip that I still had absolutely no idea how to find, but it was nice that people were willing to throw money at me regardless.

"I am certain you are quite correct. I want the Infinity memory implant from Dawson Tillet's brain."

"And in exchange for this very expensive piece of hardware? Keeping in mind that I'm legally required to secure it for my employer which—you will remember—is not you?"

Arthur returned to his seat and motioned to a second wicker sofa next to him.

"I will pay you one hundred thousand dollars for your trouble. I do hope that will make up for any potential problems with your employer?"

I didn't say anything, but my mind was spinning. With that kind of money I could pay off my debts and make a clean start. I could get away from Infinity Corp altogether if I wanted—that was assuming they didn't fire me after this mess. I might even start my own private investigation gig. It wouldn't pay as much as Infinity, but I wouldn't be running around pulling computer chips from the brains of billionaires either. That was worth a cut in pay.

I didn't want to seem too eager. I pulled a cigar from my inner jacket pocket and took out my torch lighter. "Do you mind?"

"Not at all, Mr. Malone." I offered a second cigar his way, but he held up his hand to refuse it.

I punched a hole in the cap of the cigar and then toasted the foot gently. After taking a few puffs to be sure it was lit, I returned my focus to Arthur. "I'm interested, but I need to know what I'm risking my neck for. What's so valuable about this guy's memories?"

"The sort of money I'm offering generally buys a certain degree of 'no questions asked,'" Arthur said, still smiling. It was clear he enjoyed the art of the deal. Probably because he usually came out on top. I had a feeling he could turn quite ugly when he didn't get his way. That was why he kept itchy triggermen like Walter around.

"Normally, it probably would, but you're not the only interested buyer and on top of that, I've got a dead partner that tells me this isn't as simple as it might seem."

"Your other buyers cannot afford to pay as much as I can." It was a statement and not a question. "Let me guess: a beautiful woman and an odd little man with an even more peculiar name?"

"Could be. You haven't answered my question, though. What's so valuable about this guy?"

Thomas Arthur walked over to the railing of his terrace and looked out on the Potomac and the skyline of Rosslyn beyond. I followed him and stood nearby.

"What do you see when you look out across the river, Mr. Malone?"

"My question not being answered."

Arthur laughed again. "You are a single-minded man. Please. Humor me for a moment. What do you see?"

"I see my place of employment. The Infinity Corp tower." It was at least twenty stories taller than the next-tallest building and a clear symbol of dominance that you didn't need Sigmund Freud to interpret.

"Yes, Mr. Malone. And how has Infinity risen to such wealth so quickly? What does it offer to its customers?"

I hadn't ever given it too much thought. To me it wasn't much more than vanity and hubris combined with an excess of wealth that led my future clients to pay to have a piece of hardware implanted in their brains. I'd always been a "live in the present" sort of guy and these people were always in the future. It was just one of many reasons our paths never crossed until they were lying dead in front of me.

"Conspicuous consumption. The latest gadget they can spend their money on and prove their superiority."

"There is a little bit of that, of course, but that isn't what Infinity offers. What does your employer offer?"

"Eternal life through Infinity." It was the company's motto, plastered over nearly every bit of marketing they had.

"Exactly, Mr. Malone. But we all know that is nonsense. You and I know it. Your employer knows it. And, most important of all, the customer knows it, yet he pays a large sum of money anyway. Why?"

I wasn't sure where he was going with this. "For the family. For those left behind. They can still talk, share in the good times of the past."

"Do you really think Infinity's intentions are so noble, Mr. Malone?"

I was getting sick of the chitchat and the mystery. "I don't think their intentions are noble at all. I think they want to make a buck and this is the racket they decided on. Some people sell cars. Others flip burgers. Infinity sells promises of eternal life and has a good profit margin doing so."

"Yes, sir," Thomas Arthur said. "Exactly my point. It is all business. It is all just dollars and cents in the end, isn't it?"

"And what does any of this have to do with Dawson Tillet? I'm happy to take your hundred grand in exchange for what he's got, but not if it is going to get me killed or sent to the slammer. I may not be the brightest guy around, but I know a bag of money won't do me much good if I'm in an eight-by-eight cell or six feet under. And unlike Infinity's clients, I don't give a shit about leaving something behind for my loved ones."

"Direct and to the point. That is why I like you. It is why I hire people like Walter. You and he aren't so different, I think."

"If you're looking to butter me up, you're heading down the wrong path." I didn't appreciate the comparison and I'm sure he knew it. If he thought his gun boy and I were cut from the same cloth, I was thinking he might not be such a good guy to go into business with.

"My apologies, Mr. Malone. What I meant is that you are not so burdened by seeing the world as black and white. Many people can't break that habit. They refuse to see; they refuse to acknowledge the world we live in is all shades of gray."

"That's real poetic, Mr. Arthur. Now what does it have to do with Dawson Tillet? I'm not sure if you're aware of this, but the longer it takes me to find that implant, the more the data—whatever it is you're after—is degrading. Unless you want a very expensive piece of plastic, I need to know what is so valuable so I can go get it."

"Walter." Arthur waved the young man over and he obeyed like a well-whipped hound. He stood next to us, but his eyes stayed fixed on me. He gave me the toughest look he could with bruises under his eyes and a broken nose wrapped in bandages. "Show Mr. Malone your wrist."

Walter held his hand up as though waving at me. He had my attention. "That doesn't make any sense. Why would he have—?"

"An Infinity implant? Yes, that is what the tattoo means, doesn't it?"

On Walter's wrist, right across the delicate veins and tendons was tattooed the distinctive infinity symbol of my employer, the ink shimmering as it caught the light.

"Is it real?" I asked.

"Have you heard of anyone managing to forge the tattoo?"

"No," I admitted. "The design is simple enough, but the ink is something made in house. Only a few know how they make it shift colors like that. It's how the police and medical providers know to call us in to collect from the deceased."

"Thank you, Walter. You may return to your spot."
The young man stepped back and returned his hands close
to his body, no doubt hoping to have an excuse to draw the
twin Glocks I'd seen him with earlier.

"You paid for him to be implanted?"

"Of course, Mr. Malone."

"Twenty-five million is quite a bit to spend on a two-
bit gun. What's in it for you? He family?"

"Walter is like family to me, but I have to admit that I
didn't spend so much money for reasons of sentiment. I
did it as an investment. The same reason I had Dawson
Tillet implanted. Just the same as I had Stanley Morris
implanted. And there are others beyond them."

Adding up all of the zeroes involved in that math
quickly got beyond me. Thomas Arthur was clearly bigger
money than even I had expected. I still didn't know what
his game was, but it was clear the one hundred thousand he
was offering me was chump change. I tried to catch a quick
glimpse at Arthur's wrist, but he saw it and laughed.

"No, Mr. Malone," he said, holding up his wrist for me
to examine. "I am not implanted. I have no desire to have
anyone digging into my skull, thank you."

"Alright, Arthur. I'll bite. I don't understand your
game. What do you want the memories of all these people
after they die?"

"After they die? Oh no, Mr. Malone. That is not it at
all. Of course, after they die I will check what they have,
but it is while they are living that I want them. They're
spies, Mr. Malone. All of Infinity's clients are spies, whether
they know it or not. And they all work for me."

Chapter 15

IT WAS A SHORT DRIVE from the Watergate back to the looming tower of Infinity's headquarters. I circled behind the Lincoln Memorial, still attracting visitors from around the world even as the security had tightened to oppressive levels in the city following years of both attempted and successful terrorist attacks. I could see them, fat and happy, standing along the backside of the white limestone reminder of one of our greatest presidents. What would Abraham Lincoln think about our world today? One where we no longer worried about the horrors of brother fighting against brother, but instead had traded them for religion against religion and corporation against corporation? I didn't think he would see it as an improvement.

I parked my rental a block away from Infinity, still putting together the puzzle pieces Thomas Arthur had revealed. What he'd said didn't sound possible, but I had never bothered myself with more than the bare minimum amount of knowledge about how the technology behind the Infinity memory implant functioned. I was out of my league and I needed to talk to an expert. I needed to talk to Tony Lee.

It was late in the afternoon by the time I entered Infinity. The winter sun was already very low on the horizon and the city lights were glowing. Far more people were leaving Infinity than were going in, their work for the day complete.

The guard at the desk was the same one who had called Jack and me down to meet with Selene Belle. I stopped by the counter to see if he could fill in a few blanks.

"I'm Steven Malone from Collection," I said.

"Yes, sir." It was clear he already knew my name. He probably knew the name of every employee in the building as he saw our photo and identification flash across his screen on a daily basis. I wondered how many had bothered to learn his name in return. Not many. I certainly hadn't.

"Last night my partner and I had a visitor and you called us down to speak with her. A real pretty brunette. You remember?"

I saw him swallow and his eyes dart around as though looking for a distraction, but none came. Other Infinity employees walked by us on their way out for the day but nothing that required his attention.

"Yes, sir. I remember."

"You probably heard that my partner was shot later in the night. He was killed."

"I did hear that, and I'm really sorry about that." He did seem sad. Too sad.

"Jack left with the woman that came to visit us. As far as I know, she was the last to see him. Did anything strange happen after the two of them left? Anyone else come by? Maybe someone called?"

He hesitated and looked down at his hands, but didn't speak. I read the name on his tag and did my best to be friendly.

"Ernesto? I'm not accusing you of anything. I am just trying to figure out what happened to my partner. I'm sure you understand."

He nodded. "Yes, sir, Mr. Malone. I didn't see anything. There are cameras out front, but they walked out of sight and then there wasn't anything more for me to see."

"But...?" I could tell there was more that he was holding back from me.

"Mr. Bowman called in about an hour later."

"He called you? Why would Jack call you?"

"After hours, the guard on duty handles the switchboard. He called in to the operator."

"What did he want? Why wouldn't he have just called me? I would still have been in the office at that time."

"I don't think he was calling from his own phone. At least not his work phone. The caller ID in our system didn't recognize it. He wanted to speak to you."

"I don't understand, Ernesto. Why didn't you put him through?"

"I did, Mr. Malone, but you didn't answer. I tried, but if I had known what was going to happen—"

"It's alright," I said. "You couldn't have known. Did it sound like anything was wrong? Was he panicked?"

Ernesto looked thoroughly miserable now. This had apparently been eating at him since it had happened. His eyes watered and I was afraid he was going to start attracting attention that I didn't have the patience to deal with at the moment.

"Ernesto? It wasn't your fault. If anything, it was mine, right? I stepped away from my desk and missed the call. It isn't your fault that Jack didn't get a chance to talk to anyone."

The watchman blinked and wiped away a tear. "He did, though, Mr. Malone."

"I don't follow you. He did what?"

"Mr. Bowman did talk to someone. You weren't at your desk, but someone else answered and took the call."

I had been tired last night after a long day. That combined with everything that had happened in the last twenty-four hours left things a bit of a blur. "Who took the call?"

"Mr. Lee answered. Tony Lee from Verification? He said he would take the call."

When Jack had called I'd probably just stepped away to use the toilet or grab a coffee from the vending machine. I couldn't have been gone long, but when I returned I'm certain Tony was still at his workstation processing the Stanley Morris implant. If he had spoken with my partner on the phone, why hadn't he said anything? It didn't make any sense.

"What time did Tony leave last night? Can you check that?"

Ernesto turned to his computer and pulled up the previous night's log. We all had to badge in and out of the building and everything was recorded. The security at Infinity might not be overt, but it was there and it was formidable. Ernesto looked up at me, his eyes questioning.

"Mr. Lee left immediately after you did."

—⁓—

Tony wasn't at his work space. There was someone else working there, but I didn't know him well. Manjit something or other, I think. Most of the staff in Verification shared a certain, shall we say, nerdy persuasion that made them tough to get along with if you weren't fluent in both binary and Klingon.

Manjit told me Tony hadn't been in and hadn't called. He'd missed his shift and if Manjit hadn't covered for him, he would probably have been fired. Infinity spoke highly about the importance of family and work-life balance, but they could be brutal when it came to enforcing policy. A no-show with no call in Verification was potentially a big problem. Losing data on a twenty-five-million-dollar memory implant, and the inevitable lawsuit that came with it, was unacceptable, and the fact that you couldn't be bothered to drag your flu-ridden self out of bed was no excuse. Terminated. Please bring in the next MIT grad looking for a terrific opportunity.

I stopped by my terminal and logged on to my account, but there wasn't anything of importance—a few emails of consolation about the death of Jack from the few people I actually did know around the office, other Collectors mostly, but nothing that helped in my current situation. In fact, I had an email from Human Resources requesting a meeting as soon as possible to discuss my loss. Reading between the lines, it had an Internal Affairs-style cover-your-ass smell about it. I'd seen enough of those in my police career, especially toward the end.

I rested my face in my hands and stared at the swirling color of the screen saver, considering what I knew. One, I was exhausted. I had barely slept since being called out last night for the double homicide of Dawson Tillet and Stanley Morris. If I didn't get some rest soon, I was going to fall asleep on my feet. I'd worry about that later. Sleeping wasn't going to put a hundred grand of Thomas Arthur's money in my bank account.

Two, Jack had called me last night, but Tony had spoken with him. Tony had never mentioned anything to me, so either it was nothing important, or—and I was leaning heavily toward option B—Tony wanted to keep whatever it was from me. This theory was further reinforced by the fact that Tony had left Infinity right after me, though in his email he claimed he'd been waiting for the on-call guy from Activation to come in and give him a key to the Morris implant.

Three, my partner Jack had somehow been led to the backyard of an empty house up in Cathedral Heights and then taken two rounds to the chest. Game over. Thanks for playing.

Four, everyone and their grandmother now wanted to hire me to find the missing info in Dawson Tillet's head. Information that, if Thomas Arthur was telling the truth, could be a game changer, not just for Infinity, but for the world. To see if that was possible, I needed to reach out to an expert.

I returned to the elevator and hit the button for Activation's floor. Let's see if my pal Taran Kall could clarify a few things. The same icy receptionist was at the desk. I told her I was there for Kall and she summoned him. He made me wait about ten minutes in the same small conference room as earlier in the day. I think I may have dozed off a few minutes, as he was in there before I had noticed the door open.

"Mr. Malone," Kall said as he stood over me. "I trust that you have news on the whereabouts of Mr. Tillet's memory implant?"

"I'm getting close," I said and quickly changed the subject and ignored Kall's creased brow. "I'm in need of a bit of technical assistance first. You know how complicated this stuff is to me."

"Yes, I can imagine it would be difficult to understand for someone like you."

This guy's ego almost made him too easy to manipulate. I'd swallow a bit of pride to get the job done if that was what was needed. "Is there a way to access the information on a memory implant while the client is still living?"

Taran Kall blanched visibly and took the seat next to me. You would have thought I'd just stomped on his kitten.

"What you are suggesting, Mr. Malone, is quite unethical."

"I'm not talking about ethics. I'm talking about feasibility. Is there a way to access the data while the client still lives?"

"Why would you ask such a thing?" Kall asked. A tiny bead of sweat popped up near his severe black hairline. "Did someone tell you this was possible?"

That was an interesting thing to say. Originally I thought I had hit a nerve because I had implied something unthinkable. Now it was starting to feel like it was quite the opposite. Thomas Arthur had been telling the truth. I wasn't ready to play my entire hand yet. As it was, Kall was likely to raise a few red flags after this conversation and bring additional heat on me that I didn't need.

"No, nothing like that. I just had this crazy idea that maybe someone with an Infinity implant might have seen the murder and could help us out."

Taran Kall hesitated, his eyes narrowing. "And why wouldn't we just ask this person what they saw? Why would we need to access their memories?"

"From my days on the force I know how spotty a witness's recollection can be. I thought if we could access what was saved to the implant, we'd get better information." I thought it sounded pretty good for coming from the top of my head. The fact that it wasn't too far from what Thomas Arthur claimed to be using the technology for certainly helped.

"And was there a witness to the deaths who had Infinity technology?" Kall asked.

I shrugged. "Not that I know of. I just thought it was worth looking into."

Even I thought my dodge was weak, but Taran Kall was willing to accept it. The alternative was that I knew far more than he wanted me to. I hoped the fact he had already shared some information with me against the regulations would shield me a bit from him investigating me any further. He certainly knew more than he was letting on. It wasn't some golden sense of ethics or morality that made my question to him so nerve-wracking. He thought I had found out something he wasn't ready or wasn't supposed to share.

It seemed Thomas Arthur had told me the truth. He was using people with Infinity Corp memory implants as spies. Only the most rich and powerful in the world could afford the technology and whether they knew it or not, they were sharing every second of their life with Thomas Arthur, or would be when the need arose.

Dawson Tillet was the key to Arthur's scheme. How, exactly, I didn't yet know. The man had told me just enough to keep me hunting for the missing memory implant, but not so much that I had the complete story. To be honest, I wasn't even sure I wanted to know more. Was it my place to look out for my employer? What had they ever done for me? Well, apart from hiring me when I was desperate and paying me a pretty decent wage. They did do that.

But if Taran Kall knew there could be some sort of other use for the memory implant, and his reaction seemed to indicate he knew something, then perhaps Infinity wasn't the victim in all of this.

"I would suggest you leave your imagination out of the investigation, Mr. Malone. What about the image I provided to Tony Lee? What about this memory of 'the Hun'? Didn't that provide any leads for you?"

"Speaking of Tony," I said, dodging the question, "how much information would your temporary passkey allow access to? I haven't been able to track Tony down today to ask him."

"Why, all of it. The pass we provided was a 'temporary' one, not a 'partial' one. Whoever used that pass would have had full access to the client's memories, but only for about an hour before the key was no longer accepted. Of course, a freshly retrieved memory implant does require a bit of finesse from the Activation department to be fully accessible. That would be well beyond someone from Verification, but Mr. Lee would have been able to gain quite a bit of information."

That didn't line up with what I'd been told by Tony. I decided that was strike three against my Verification colleague. The first was not telling me about Jack's call and the second was lying about his whereabouts last night. Now I had found out he had full access to Morris's memories and hadn't informed me. It was hard to come to any conclusion other than that Tony had learned something important from the implant. Important enough to kill Jack? I didn't want to believe that, but I'd seen enough in my life to never discount anyone's ability to commit murder given enough incentive. I needed to find him.

"Huh, I never knew that."

"Mr. Malone, did you really stop by here just to ask about things you could never really understand?" Taran Kall stared at me. He gave me a flash of perfect teeth. One of these days I wasn't going to need anything from him, and I was going to crack a few of those pearly whites for him. "You need to be out there finding our missing memory implant. There are family members desperate to contact their loved one."

I knew there were people desperate for Dawson Tillet's implant, but it wasn't any family members. I wasn't likely to get much more out of Activation. My gut told me someone in his office had committed a major screw-up by giving Tony Lee that activation key. Now they were desperate to see Tillet recovered to cover their tracks.

"You're probably right, Mr. Kall. I was just in the office checking on some other leads and thought I'd run my idea by you. I see now that it was stupid."

I got up and walked out without another word to him. I gave the receptionist a wink on the way out just to see her scowl back at me. It'd been a tough day, but riling these folks up was almost as good as playing trifecta on a sure thing.

Chapter 16

I WAS STARTING TO GET a feel for the *why* in this story, but the *how* and the *who* were still eluding me. There's one rule of detective work that you learn quickly: when you're stuck on a case, always go back to the beginning. Retrace your steps. Talk to the same people. See what shakes loose the second time around. I decided it was time to head to the scene of the crime, the alleyway where Dawson Tillet and Stanley Morris had met their grisly ends. I hoped that there might be something I'd missed. Something that gave me a direction.

Although it was only early evening, the winter sun had long since set and I found the alley dark just as it had been the night before. The crime scene was already cleaned up, and apart from a slightly darker bit of stone there was no evidence to indicate two men had been murdered here just a short time ago. The neighborhood was a nice one full of lively restaurants and bars with tourists admiring

Christmas-themed store displays. A double homicide wouldn't play well here and the police knew it.

After a quick glance around, I moved from the busy street into the alley. It was rather narrow and made more so by a row of dumpsters that probably belonged to the neighboring cafe. The alley opened on the other end to a small parking lot which connected to a parallel street. I looked around, trying to determine what had brought the two men here.

According to Thomas Arthur, Tillet had worked for him as a spy. His job was to get into places where security was tight and simply take everything in as quickly as possible before being tossed out. What he witnessed might be too fleeting for him to properly understand, but it wasn't too quick for his Infinity memory implant to record. Arthur then took advantage of his hacking of the technology to find out what Tillet knew.

That was one account of what was going on. If Selene Belle were to be believed—and that was a pretty big if—Dawson Tillet had been her lover and his memories, if recovered, would spell disaster for her with her dangerous husband. It wasn't clear where Stanley Morris figured into that scenario other than Selene had said Dawson had gone undercover for a meeting.

I wondered if both could be telling the truth. Could it be Dawson Tillet was both spying for Thomas Arthur and sleeping with Selene Belle? It was plausible. Perhaps she was the target? I didn't have enough information to know. I was receiving contradictory stories about Dawson Tillet's importance, but so far no one had shed any light on Stanley Morris. Who was he? Why did he have an Infinity Corp implant? If he was another spy of Arthur's, surely the rich man would have said something.

I checked the alleyway, but found no signs of video surveillance. Of course not. That would have made things too easy. There wasn't anything in the alley that seemed worth protecting. The parking lot at the end didn't have any obvious cameras and neither did the busy street on the other end. It wouldn't have helped me much at any rate. The police would have already checked and if there was video, they would have already seen it.

From the street the alley was quite dark. There was a light near the entrance, but it didn't seem to work. It would have made a good location for a quick, clandestine meeting. Going by the recovered image from Morris's implant, Dawson Tillet had pulled a gun on him. That didn't mean he'd necessarily shot him, but it was definitely possible. Both had been killed by a needle gun—rare and distinctive. The fuzzy image from the memory wasn't sharp enough to tell if Tillet had the flechette pistol. The police would have looked for the murderous little needles that had shredded the insides of Tillet and Morris. It was impossible to pull any sort of forensics from them, though.

Looking around to see who might have had a good view of the alley brought me to a small independent bookstore across the street. The place was cramped with shelves and stacks of books occupying every inch of space. A small counter was near the front window, and a clerk sat on a chair behind it. From there one would have had a great view across the street into the alley.

When you think of a used bookstore, you often picture a slender professorial type wearing a worn sweater and thick glasses. That was the exact opposite of the clerk at Into the Breach Books. The man behind the counter was black, with a shaved head, and had to be at least 250 pounds of muscle. He fixed me with a hard look when I entered, as though the very idea of customers bothered him.

"Were you working last night?" I asked and slid over a business card identifying me as a Collector for Infinity

Corp. For some people, it worked almost as well as a badge, but not for this guy.

He didn't touch my card, barely glanced at it before sighing and carefully marking his place in his book—*The Man in the High Castle* by Philip K. Dick. "I work here every night. It's my place."

"There were two men killed in the alley across the way last night," I said and paused. He didn't say anything. "I was hoping you might have seen something."

"I already spoke with the police. One of the victims a client of yours?"

He was quick and to the point. I knew I could deal with this guy. "Both of them, actually."

"I didn't realize it fell within your job description to also solve the murders of your clients. I thought you just uploaded their consciousness into a video game."

I chuckled. "Not a fan of Infinity technology, I take it?"

"I say live and let live. When I was a kid I remember a few eccentric billionaires having their heads chopped off and frozen in hopes of immortality. If your clients want to be turned into Wikipedia, it's no sweat off my back."

"I'm with you. I'm just a cog in the machine, trying to do my job."

He nodded but arched his eyebrows as though he didn't understand my career choice. If he only knew. "Anyway, like I told the police, I didn't see anything."

"Alright. Forget about last night. What about the alley in general? Anything unusual about it? Drug dealers? Prostitutes? Mormon missionaries? I'll take anything at this point."

"I really can't help you, man. It's a pretty safe neighborhood. Definitely never had anything like this happen." The clerk started to pick up his book, obviously done with me and ready to get back to his dystopian science fiction.

I pulled the print out from my pocket of the last image Stanley Morris saw before being shot. "What about this guy? You ever seen him?"

The clerk sat his book back down and looked at the photo in front of him. "Is this the killer? What is that, surveillance footage?"

"Something like that. Recognize him?"

"He does look a bit familiar. The quality isn't too good." The clerk brought the photo closer to his face for a better look. "Yeah, I have seen that guy. He was in here just a few days ago."

It was something. Whatever Dawson Tillet was up to, perhaps he had used this same bookstore to surveil the location across the way. It's what I would have done if I was meeting someone I didn't know much about in a dark alley.

"Did you talk to him?" I asked.

"Not really. Just rang up his purchase. We didn't chat. He didn't seem that talkative and I wasn't out to make a friend."

"He bought something? Do you have a record of what he purchased?"

"Yeah, the record is right here." The clerk tapped the side of his head. "I don't make so many sales that I can't remember them for a while. I ain't in this business for the money."

With a quick look around, it was clear he was telling the truth. This had all the hallmarks of a hobby business. This was probably this guy's own personal collection. I wouldn't be surprised if he brought in more books than actually went out.

"What did this man buy?"

"*English Hunting Dogs.*"

I wasn't sure I heard him correctly. "I'm sorry. Did you say—?"

"Yep. That was it. It is a big photo book. You know, like a coffee table type book. About this big by this big." The clerk held his hands about twelve and then eighteen inches apart. "Nice book. Good condition."

"Was it valuable?" I asked.

"Not really. Forty bucks is what I sold it for. It might have been worth fifty, maybe sixty to the right buyer."

It didn't really help me. Maybe it didn't mean anything. It could just be that Dawson Tillet was a fan of dogs. I like cats. They aren't so needy. I don't think it would give anyone a particular psychological insight into me. I'd learned in my days as a detective that sometimes the answer is "just because." Then again, sometimes the littlest things hold the most importance. I filed this little bit away and hoped it might help down the road.

"Anything else you can remember about the guy? Ever seen him before that or since?"

The clerk pushed the photo back toward me. "Nope. That was it. Sorry I can't help any more." He picked up his book and opened it to his bookmark without waiting to see if I was done asking questions.

"Alright. Thanks." I turned to walk out of the shop and stopped. "Did you tell the police any of this? About the guy coming in for the book?"

"Nope," the clerk said without looking up from his book. "They didn't show me that picture. So whatever it is you and your company are doing to cover its tracks, you're one step ahead of the police."

I took a seat on a bench in front of the bookstore and across from the alley. I pulled a Montecristo number two from my inner jacket pocket, clipped it, and lit it with my Ronson. Of all my vices, strangely enough it was the cigars that hadn't hurt me yet. The gambling and the drinking had done more than their share, but a bit of Cuban tobacco in a Maduro wrapper had yet to betray me. A little voice in my head told me I'd probably get cancer. I did my best to ignore it.

I did some of my best thinking with a cigar in hand and I could use all the help I could get. I could feel the threads of an idea starting to weave together in the back of my mind, but they weren't yet fully formed enough for me to grab onto. This whole mess didn't make any sense. The two dead clients, Jack getting murdered, Tony Lee lying to me and now nowhere to be found, and far too many people looking to throw money at the problem to make it go away.

As much as I could use the cash, I was smart enough to know that step one for the rich and powerful was to throw money at a problem. If that didn't work, step two usually involved making the problem disappear. Dawson Tillet had already disappeared—at least, the part of him that anyone seemed to care about—but I was still around and I had a feeling I might know more than certain parties wanted. Jack Bowman's death could have been a pre-emptive warning shot. Could be whoever did that didn't need two Collectors to work for them; one would do and the other would serve as incentive. Jack had drawn the short end of the straw.

I was only about an inch into the cigar when an un-marked police cruiser pulled up across the street. I watched as Detective Thorsen exited the passenger seat and took a quick look around. His eyes swept over me, but he didn't give any indication he recognized me in the dark shadows of the winter evening. After a second, the engine turned off, and Sergeant Valentine pulled his bulk out from behind the steering wheel and adjusted his belt and sidearm. He didn't have Thorsen's concern for situational awareness and barely avoided being nicked by a passing car. He shouted a profanity at the driver as it went by.

I guess I'm not the only one going back to square one, I thought to myself. It was unusual that Thorsen had Valentine tagging along, though. Maybe since he was the new kid on the block, this was some sort of hazing. I could barely tolerate Valentine from a distance, and I couldn't imagine riding around all day with him. He was a blunt instrument, and detective work required precision tools.

I watched as they both entered the dark alley. With a moonless night and the glare of street lamps casting heavy shadows, I couldn't make out what they did in the alley, but I saw a small circle of crisp white light snap on and dart around as Thorsen took another look at the scene. It was unlikely the crime scene techs had left anything behind, but sometimes going through the motions can jar a thought loose. Even from my seat, I could hear Valentine's gruff voice cut through the air, though I couldn't make out the words over the low noise of the street traffic. He sounded like he was complaining. It was cold and probably well past the end of the sergeant's shift. In my day there'd been plenty like him on the force, only there for the perks of the occasional free food, the chance to bully teenagers, and a future pension. Since I'd left, I think the number of Valentines policing the city had only gone up.

Thorsen saw me coming before I got to them, the glow of my cigar a beacon in the dark night. "Funny seeing you here, Malone," he said as he shook my hand.

"Back to the scene of the crime, Rocket? Afraid you left some evidence behind?" Valentine laughed at his own joke.

"If you think I had something to do with this, then I'm not surprised you haven't made any progress."

"We don't believe you were involved with the murders, Malone," Thorsen said before Valentine could speak. "Isn't that right, Sergeant?"

Valentine shrugged his meaty shoulders. "If you say so, Detective. All I know is that we arrived to a crime scene to find a criminal standing there. Seems like a pretty easy case to me."

I took a step toward Valentine, but Thorsen held up an arm between us. "Let it go. Both of you. We all want to find out what happened here. This isn't helping."

It was childish to let Sergeant Valentine get to me. He was a blowhard and an idiot to boot. Knowing that a cop as pathetic as him was still on the force when I'd been kicked to the curb stung, even years later. I may have been dirty technically, but I'd never hurt anyone. I did a good job. It was never my sense of justice that was a problem; it was just a matter of cashflow. I had more flowing out, mostly to bookies like Attila, than coming in. If I could shake down the occasional small-time crack dealer for a few bucks, I didn't see an impact on the bottom line. Who was hurt? Just a few crackheads who were buying.

"My company's getting hot to make some progress on finding this missing implant," I said to Thorsen. "How is the investigation coming? Anything promising?"

"I think we're moving in the right direction, but it is slow going. Something shady was definitely going on. Victim one—Stanley Morris—is practically a ghost. A few hits from years back, but then he just fell off the radar. No known family or next of kin. Last known location was London, though we think he's American. Even that is uncertain."

It made sense to me. If Morris was one of Arthur's cyber spies, he would probably have been living most of his life in the dark. It might also explain why Morris and Tillet had been meeting in this alley. If they were both spies in Arthur's employ, so perhaps this was some sort of trade of information or a job they were working on together. Could be Tillet betrayed Morris and shot him—over what, I didn't have any theories on, but in that line of work, bad things happened. It was all conjecture, though, and nothing I was ready to share with Detective Thorsen and Sergeant Valentine. Also, it still had one big hole: who killed Tillet?

"Anyone from Infinity Corp legal division been in touch with you yet?" I asked. "They should be able to pull some good info from Morris's implant, but it often takes a day or two to get everything set up."

"Someone did reach out, but it's like you said. Nothing yet. I'll check back with them tomorrow."

I nodded and flicked the ash off my cigar. "It should do a lot to fill in the blanks. What about Tillet?"

"Who?" Thorsen asked.

I motioned with my cigar to where the headless body had lain. Under the light of Thorsen's flashlight, the dark stain from the pool of blood could still be seen, bits of red soaked into the crevices between the bricks. "Dawson Tillet. Our decapitated friend."

Thorsen tilted his head at an angle and looked at me funny. I realized I hadn't actually filled the police in on the ID of the second body. Certainly they would have figured that out by now, though, through prints or DNA. For that matter, the guy might have had a wallet on him.

"Who's Dawson Tillet?" Thorsen asked. Valentine rejoined us from the car, suddenly interested in the conversation. I was afraid I had just screwed something up.

"I'm sorry, Detective Thorsen. I guess I forgot to give you the name of the second guy. I got pretty distracted with my partner getting shot later in the night. I figured you would have identified him by now, though. Dawson Tillet was our second victim. He of the missing head." I tried to keep it light, but I didn't like the way either of the police officers were looking at me. Either I knew too much or I didn't know as much as I thought I did. Both could be a serious problem.

"Looks like you ain't Mr. Knows Everything after all," Valentine said. "I'm surprised—"

"How did you get the victim's identity?" Thorsen said, stepping in front of Valentine.

Now I was in a rough spot. Detective Thorsen was too smart for me to pull a fast one on. I could have pushed Sergeant Valentine off the Memorial Bridge into the Potomac River and still convinced him he was standing in the middle of the National Mall, but Thorsen was smart.

Was he upset because I had identified Tillet without informing him? That didn't feel right. It might have annoyed him a bit, but he'd still be thankful for the tip, even if it came late. As it was, he should have already figured it out on his own if he was half the detective I pegged him for. Still, he was clearly bothered by something.

I realized my blunder. There really wasn't any good way for me to know Dawson Tillet's identity. It wasn't like I could run prints or DNA analysis. Jack Bowman and I were called to the scene because the cops had two dead bodies with Infinity tattoos on their wrists. It was standard protocol. I hadn't learned who Stanley Morris was until I pulled his implant and scanned it. I hadn't been able to do that with Tillet. A good detective—and Thorsen was that—would reason the only way I could have known who the body belonged to was if someone told me, or I was the killer.

"Mr. Malone?" Thorsen repeated. "I asked you a question. How do you know this is Dawson Tillet?" He'd always been cordial with me. Not quite friendly, but respectful and professional, probably due to both his nature and my former position. It was more than I ever received from the old-timers like Valentine. That tone had slipped away and was replaced with determination. If I didn't come up with a good answer now, I'd be talking all night in the precinct.

"We had a call from the family. Obviously someone with an Infinity implant disappears and we get a call in case the worst has come to be. I thought the legal section would have passed that along."

"When did this call come in?" Thorsen asked.

"I can't recall exactly," I said. "I'm sorry to have left you in the dark, but I figured you knew. Look, I've been real busy between this case and Jack's death—"

"There's just one problem, Mr. Malone," Thorsen said. "The second deceased wasn't Dawson Tillet. His name was Ryan Middleton."

I didn't know what to say. Had Selene played me? If she had, so had Mr. China and Thomas Arthur. Were they all working together? It didn't make any sense.

"I don't understand, Thorsen," I said. "Why would—?"

"I think we'd better continue this conversation at the precinct, if you don't mind."

"Is that a request?" I asked. I'd been through the game enough times to know it wasn't.

"It is right now, but if you refuse I'm afraid it may turn into something more."

"Please, Rocket," Valentine said, his wide grin visible even in the darkness of the alley. "Please resist. It would make my entire fuckin' year."

I ignored him and walked to their car. When Thorsen opened the back door, I got in the sedan, already lost in the maelstrom of thoughts and events of the day.

Chapter 17

THE COFFEE WAS AWFUL—brown water with little clumps of powdered creamer that refused to dissolve no matter how forcefully stirred. Bits of the styrofoam cup could be mixed in with the creamer and I wouldn't know the difference. I was exhausted, nearly dead on my feet, and this swill wasn't going to keep me going.

"Any chance of real coffee? Instant is an assault on human decency."

Detective Thorsen had a cup of the same in front of him, but hadn't touched it. For him it was just a prop used by police to make interviews seem more like friendly conversations. Despite the lack of handcuffs and an actual arrest, I knew this wasn't a monthly meeting of the neighborhood book club. I was in trouble and it didn't matter how good a guy Thorsen had seemed before. If he thought I was holding back information about his double murder, he wasn't going to go easy on me. He had done an admirable job of giving me a fair shake despite all the noise I am sure he heard about my past from Sergeant Valentine and his cronies. Still, there was open-minded and there was naive.

"Sorry, Malone," Thorsen said. "It seems our barista has the night off. Tell me again about Dawson Tillet."

I hadn't spilled Selene Belle's name yet. Hers or any of the other players. It wasn't that I was protecting them—well, maybe Selene a bit—they weren't anything to me. I wasn't covering for any of them, but I also didn't need the police looking too closely into what was going on. Once I understood what was really going on—and I'd been paid—I'd help Thorsen out. At this point, I only knew enough to know I didn't know damn well enough to feel secure.

"Look, Thorsen," I said. "I know how the game is played, but I can't keep giving you the same story over and over again. If we're done, I've got places I can be."

"Let's stop playing games, then, Malone. Stop telling stories and start telling the truth. We've identified the second victim as Ryan Middleton, age fifty-seven, from McLean, Virginia. Both the prints and DNA confirm it. Clearly you thought the body was someone by the name of Tillet. Why did you think that? Who told you that?"

"Like I said, someone called in to Infinity Corp and reported it. The company—including Jack and I—assumed that the other body had to be Dawson Tillet. I guess we were wrong. I don't see what the big deal is."

"The big deal is that you withheld information from me," Thorsen said, leaning closer across the cold plastic laminate table between us. "I thought we were working together. I've treated you right, Malone."

I held up my hands as though warding off his words. "You have. I admit that. I should have told you about the ID I had, even though it turned out to be wrong. I'm not trying to derail your case. We're still looking for the same thing: The head from that body."

"No," Thorsen said. "You're looking for the head. Infinity Corp is looking for its property. What I am looking for is the killer of two men."

"Three men," I said quietly.

"What?" Thorsen asked.

"Three men. Jack Bowman. My partner? Let's not forget about him."

Thorsen softened, his shoulders relaxed. "I haven't, Malone. And I'm sorry about that, but I'm talking about the double homicide in the alley."

"I think Jack Bowman's murder has to be connected."

"What makes you say that? Different murder weapon. Different neighborhood. No obvious connection to the other two victims apart from Infinity. If you've got something—"

"Just my gut," I said. "But you're a detective. You know that's something. And I wouldn't be so quick to discount the Infinity Corp connection. Jack and I were both working the case and it seems to me whoever took Tillet— I mean, Middleton's head wanted to hide that data. I can't imagine they'd have any problems killing Jack or me to keep it quiet."

"But what did Jack know? Why'd the killer go after him?"

It was a good question and I didn't have a real good answer. I hadn't mentioned Selene Belle yet and it was possible that she didn't have anything to do with it, but I didn't know. Detective Thorsen was right, though. I did owe him something. Besides, I had so many lines in the water at this point, if I got a bite I probably wouldn't even notice. Maybe I could get the police to take up some slack and do a little legwork for me.

"Alright, Thorsen," I said. "I might have something."

The detective opened his mouth to speak and I could see a bit of heat coming to his cheeks.

"Don't start on me," I said before he could talk. "I swear to God I just found this out before I ran into you guys and I didn't think it meant anything, but now I'm not so sure." That was about eighty percent true. I'd always take those sort of odds.

"What do you have?" Thorsen had his pen to his notebook, ready for anything I might offer.

I gave the detective a slightly redacted version of what had happened after I met him in the alley that night. I told him how Jack and I had returned to headquarters and encouraged Tony Lee to rush the verification so that we could help the police find the location of the second implant. I left out the part about our visit from Selene Belle and her offer of ten grand each to slow the investigation—that would have damned me for sure—but I mentioned Jack's call after he left and how Tony took the call without mentioning it.

"You think your partner left a message with this…" Thorsen said, checking over his notes. "This Tony Lee guy?"

"That's exactly what I think, but Tony never even told me Jack called. Now normally that might not mean much. Tony is usually head first in a few computer monitors and only communicates with Jack and me as much as the job requires. He could easily have forgotten to pass on the message."

"Then why are you telling me this?" Thorsen asked.

"Because I checked the logs with the security guard and Tony left Infinity right after I did that night, but he was supposed to be there all night working on the implant from Morris. I told him it could be important for the police. In fact, I had an email from him the next morning and he said he'd been there for hours, waiting on someone from another office to pass him some info he needed."

"So where did Tony Lee go?" Thorsen asked.

"Exactly. And where has he been? Because he hasn't been back to work since."

That made Thorsen look up from his notebook. "Well, that is odd, isn't it?"

"I thought so."

"You think Tony Lee could have killed your partner?" Thorsen asked.

I furrowed my brow at the question. I didn't know what I thought. "Honestly, I'm not sure. Jack and I sort of needled him a bit, but we didn't really know him all that well. He thought he was much smarter than us. Smarter than everyone, really, and he is, probably, but I have a hard time seeing him killing someone. I guess it depends on what Jack told him on the phone."

"I thought most of you Collectors came from law enforcement backgrounds. Hard to believe a lab tech could take you out."

"Jack came from the army. He was infantry so definitely no slouch, but my days on the force taught me that a bullet tends to beat most training. Two will do it even better, especially if you're not expecting it."

"Like if it was coming from a co-worker," Detective Thorsen said. "I will have some folks check into it. We'll go by his place and see if he's been there. If we're lucky, we'll find a frozen head in the freezer. I wish I could say it would be the first time. I take it you haven't been by?"

"Infinity isn't your usual office job. They discourage socialization among the staff. It's all secrets and mysteries there. Tony wasn't exactly the sort of guy I'd share a beer with normally, but even if I wanted to, I don't know where he lives."

"Infinity will tell me or I'll have a judge sign a warrant for the information," Thorsen said.

I didn't respond, but I knew it wouldn't necessarily be so easy despite the detective's tough talk. Infinity had a lot of money and powerful clients. Both of those things could buy a lot of sway with the judicial system. If there was anything that Infinity hated, it was bad press.

"Listen, Detective Thorsen," I said. "It's been a long and, frankly, pretty damn awful stretch of hours. I just want to go home and get some sleep. Unless you want to charge me with misidentifying a dead guy, I'd like to go."

For a moment I thought he wasn't going to let me leave the station. I thought he would charge me, that I'd damaged our budding relationship too much. What he could lay on me, I had no idea. Although I'd spent my day with an entire Broadway ensemble of disreputable characters, as far as I recalled, I hadn't done anything illegal. That doesn't always mean much to some police. Luckily, Thorsen wasn't one of those guys.

"Alright, you can go. Just do me a favor and stay in town the next few days. In case we have more questions."

"I'll cancel my Cancun all-inclusive," I said, standing. My legs were stiff from the uncomfortable chair and my stomach gave a bit of a lurch. I didn't know if it was from hunger or the instant sludge I'd been sipping from that cup.

As I was leaving the small room—an interrogation room, if you wanted to be particular—I passed Sergeant Valentine on his way back in. His face scrunched up into a piglike scowl that caused his mustache to stick out like a brush. He knew Thorsen had let me walk. I don't know why he'd expected anything different. They didn't have me on anything, even obstruction.

"Next time I see you," I told him, slapping a hand on his shoulder, "it'll be far too soon. You take care now, Sergeant Valentine."

He shrugged my hand off his shoulder and puffed out his chest. "I think we'll be talking again real soon and you won't be so smug next time. You're no good, Rocket. It's only a matter of time before you end up locked up like the rest of the scum."

I had a good poker face and I certainly wasn't going to reveal too much to the likes of Valentine, but even I had to admit, at least to myself, that I felt a small stab of doubt right in my gut. It felt like he was right. I would end up here again if I wasn't careful. I don't know what I feared more: ending up in jail or Sergeant Valentine having his opinion about my worth validated.

Chapter 18

I LEFT THE STATION AND realized my rental car was still parked at the crime scene. It was late and cold, and I was damn near sleeping on my feet, but I knew I had to retrieve the car. I'd want it in the morning and if I made my way home without it tonight, I'd just be pissed off when I woke up. I didn't have any cash since Ladykiller Lou and Sergei had wiped me out the night before so I stopped at an ATM a block away.

The cop in me usually avoided using the money machines because it seemed a prime way to get held up. When I felt the cold steel of a gun barrel jam into my side, I almost laughed. Of course. This is how my day was going. I didn't move and I didn't say anything. The last thing I needed was my big mouth earning me a bullet by a strung-out tweaker for two hundred bucks.

"Don't move, Mr. Malone." The voice was familiar, nasal like its owner had a bad cold. I felt another hand pat down my jacket and waist looking for a gun that I didn't have. "We're going for a little ride."

Now that I knew it wasn't a crackhead after my cash, I turned to find Walter, Thomas Arthur's hired gun, standing next to me. His hand was in the pocket of his duster, but the gun pushed forward into my floating ribs. I knew it was the real deal under the jacket. After all, I'd already taken the heaters from him once today. He was probably itching to use them on me now, but I knew he wouldn't without his employer's blessing.

"Walter, isn't it?" I said, smiling. "Funny meeting you here. Don't tell me you've been following me again, because last time that—"

He was quicker than I expected. The gun poking into my ribs barely moved, but his left snaked out fast in a quick rabbit punch to my gut. For a moment I thought I was going to lose my instant coffee all over the ATM, but instead I found myself sucking air and trying to stay conscious. I took a step back to put a little distance between us, not normally a good idea when facing an armed opponent, but I didn't think he was going to shoot. He just wanted payback, but I wasn't going to give it to him easy.

But I was exhausted and I'd underestimated him based on his earlier performance. I thought he was nothing without those twin Glocks, but it turned out the kid could handle himself. I shifted my weight back on my heels and then launched forward again with my right, but I was crowded by the wall the ATM was built into and couldn't get a good angle. He deflected my blow easily with his left hand and with a smooth motion pulled his right out of his jacket pocket, with the handgun still in it. He whipped it up and the butt of the handle connected with my jaw. All I saw was a flash of starlight and the wet asphalt coming up to quickly meet my face.

—∭—

When I came to I didn't know where I was. I was lying on a couch—a chaise lounge, technically—of good quality. A fire burned in a small fireplace and a terrible likeness of a nude woman hung over the mantel. It was bad enough that I assumed it had cost a small fortune. I swung my legs around and sat up too quickly. For a moment I had to brace myself on the gray velvet edge of the sofa to avoid collapsing back onto it. My head felt like a jackhammer had been used for a bit of neurosurgery. I touched my jaw and found a small knot that made me suck air involuntarily just by coming near it.

"You're awake," a voice said. "How very good. I do apologize for Walter's behavior. I am afraid, however, that you brought that at least partially on yourself. You were quite rude to him last time."

I turned to see Thomas Arthur sitting on a nearby chair and drinking a glass of wine. He was wearing a tuxedo and appeared more ready for a night at the opera than to be interrogating a man he'd just had knocked out and dragged into his rented flat. I glanced around the room and there was no sign of Walter. That was probably good for both of us. I knew I'd take a go at him, but in my current condition I didn't think I'd fare much better than last time. I promised myself he'd never get another sucker punch in on me. I thought I had taught the kid a lesson the first time we met, but it didn't seem to have stuck. I would have to be more emphatic next time.

"Mr. Arthur," I said slowly, the words making my head hurt even more than I thought possible, "I've had a very long day and I just want to go to bed."

"Yes, yes. I am quite sure of that. It's just that you are supposed to be finding something for me. Instead, I find you at the police station. You can see how that might be of concern, right? I thought it was understood that when I offered you one hundred thousand dollars of my hard-earned money to find Dawson Tillet, I meant without the help of the police. After all, I already own enough police officers. What I want is your help."

There was a small table at the end of the chaise lounge with a glass and a pitcher of ice water. I helped myself and took a quick sip, then held the cool glass against my aching head. The steel-toed kicks to my temple eased into the gentle stomp of a tennis shoe on my skull.

"I didn't go to the police," I said slowly. "I was picked up by the police for questioning. It wasn't exactly an invitation. Besides, I didn't say anything about you."

"And they let you go? Why did they do that?" Arthur asked. He kept his voice conversational, inquisitive, but I understood the implication.

"Because they've got nothing on me. I didn't do anything. I didn't kill those men. I don't know who did. To be honest, I don't even care who killed them. I'm just trying to find the missing implant. That's what you want, right?"

"Yes, quite," he said, taking a drink of his wine. "But it isn't the only thing. I always want you to understand something, Mr. Malone."

I didn't like where this was going. "And what's that?"

"I want you," Thomas Arthur said, the friendly tone falling away, replaced by iron, "to understand that you work for me now. Whether you find Dawson Tillet or one of the many other people in my employ finds him makes no difference to me. What matters is that everyone remembers their place."

"Now wait a minute, Arthur," I said, headache searing as my voice rose. I ignored it. "I don't belong to anyone. Not to Infinity. Not to the police. And certainly not to you. You want to pay me a hundred grand to find something.

Fine. I'll find it. But that's a business arrangement. Nothing more and nothing less. And it's something I can't do if your lap dog is following me around and dragging me to the Watergate every damn time you want to have a chat."

I pulled myself to my feet and did my best not to sway. I think I was mostly successful. I closed my eyes for a moment to allow the room to stop spinning. "Now, unless you've got something to add that will actually help me find Dawson Tillet, I'm leaving."

I took two heavy steps toward the door, but it felt like I didn't get any closer. I hoped to make this exit look impressive without collapsing onto my face. That kid had really put everything he had into that blow to my jaw. Maybe I had just gotten a bit soft over the years since I'd left the force.

"Mr. Malone," Thomas Arthur said from his seat. "Who do you think killed Jack Bowman?"

I stopped and turned back to him. He took a casual drink from his wine and looked at the fire as though I wasn't even in the room with him. Anger brought the spinning room back into sharp focus and I took a step toward him.

"Is that supposed to be a threat?" I asked. "You killed my partner? Or one of your goons, I should say. You'd never have the courage to do it yourself."

"Your problem, Mr. Malone," he said, "is that you seem to have trouble selecting the correct people to trust."

I sat back down on the chaise lounge, though I didn't recall making a conscious decision to do so. "What does that mean?"

He raised his voice and called out. "Please come in."

A door to the room opened from behind me and I spun in the awkward piece of furniture to see who it was. I hoped it would be Walter. He and I had some things to discuss, but it wasn't him.

Mr. China also wore formalwear, a tuxedo of midnight blue with black satin lapels. A small white daisy was in the boutonniere hole of his jacket and he smiled when he saw me. The smile didn't lie well on his gaunt undertaker's features. It made him look like a skull dressed for the opera.

"Good evening, Mr. Malone," he said in that strangely accented whisper of his. "How good to see you."

It was obviously some sort of display of power on Thomas Arthur's part, but I didn't really get it. In the last day it seemed everyone and their mother was looking for the man supposedly known as Dawson Tillet and they had all come to me for help. Was I supposed to be surprised that they were all connected in some way?

"Am I supposed to be shocked that you two know each other?" I said to Thomas Arthur, ignoring China's greeting. "Because I really don't care and I don't see what it has to do with Jack Bowman's murder."

Then I remembered the gun I had taken from Mr. China the first time we met. I turned to face him, my eyebrows drawing in tight together. He suddenly stopped moving toward me and held up his hands.

"No, Mr. Malone, I did—"

"Mr. China did not kill Jack Bowman," Arthur said, cutting him off. "My point is this: You seem to have trouble differentiating the good guys from the bad guys."

I couldn't help but laugh, a harsh bark with no humor behind it. "I see. And you two are the good guys?"

Mr. China continued walking and took a seat near us, apparently feeling more confident that I wasn't about to throttle him for the murder of my partner. Thomas Arthur shrugged and raised his eyebrows.

"I suppose you could say good and bad is relative," he said.

143

"Alright, I'll bite," I said. "What does any of this have to do with Jack's death? If you guys didn't do it, then who did?"

"I think you already know the answer to that question, Mr. Malone," Thomas Arthur said.

"I told you she couldn't be trusted," Mr. China said. "You only see her sad eyes and big breasts. She is using you, just the same as she uses everyone."

"Selene Belle?" I asked. "Why would she kill my partner? What is there to gain from that? She hired us to find Dawson Tillet. The same as you." I pointed to Mr. China. "And the same as you." I pointed to Thomas Arthur.

"That is a question you should pose to Ms. Belle," Thomas Arthur said. "Should you ever see her again. She has a way of disappearing and taking things with her of which she has no ownership."

I smiled, despite the pain in my head. "Ah, I see now. She played you. She played both of you. And now you want me to do your dirty work for you. That's rich." I laughed, but neither of the two men seemed to see the humor in the situation.

"Mr. Malone," Thomas Arthur said. "I do not know what game Selene Belle is playing, but I can assure you that I am not a part of it. My deal still stands. One hundred thousand dollars for the memory implant in Dawson Tillet's brain. Whatever she is offering you is all smoke and mirrors."

"And what about your fifty grand?" I asked Mr. China. "How does that factor in?"

He smiled bashfully and adjusted his bow tie. "I must admit that I never had such a large sum of money to pay you. I thought I would deal with that hurdle when I came to it, but now that I have come to an arrangement with Mr. Arthur, it is no longer a concern."

"Right," I said, sick of talking to the weird foreigner. Nothing he said made sense to me. I stood up, and the dizziness didn't come back. I was feeling a bit better.

"You just leave Selene Belle to me," I told Arthur. "And you tell your sidekick that he'd better keep clear. I've never been a man for unnecessary violence, but that is more a guideline than a rule. I'm happy to make an exception for him."

I didn't wait for any sort of dismissal. If Thomas Arthur wanted to keep me here, he was going to have to do it with force, but nothing happened. He also seemed smart enough to keep Walter and me from running into each other on my way out.

I left the Watergate and flagged a taxi out front to take me back to my rental car. On the way, I remembered to check my wallet and found five hundred dollars in it. I didn't remember actually getting any money out of the ATM so it must have been a down payment from Thomas Arthur, a little reminder that I worked for him.

Chapter 19

THE LAST THING I REMEMBERED was relief that my rental car was still in one piece. I more than half expected to find it had been redesigned by Sergei as a reminder from Attila about my quickly approaching deadline. Fortunately, that hadn't happened. I must have driven home in a state that was completely unsafe to other drivers, pedestrians, and parked cars. Luckily it was late enough that most everyone else on the road was probably drunk and didn't notice.

I awoke fully dressed in my bed to someone pounding on my front door. My apartment was bright-I had apparently neglected to turn off any lights before crashing. Outside it was still dark. That, combined with my lingering exhaustion, convinced me the time on my clock must be correct: 4:27 a.m. The knock on the door had grown quieter in the few seconds it took me to get there, but still continued. I thought it had been going on a while before it had finally woken me.

A quick check through the peephole revealed an empty hallway, but I could still hear knocking. It came from near the floor. I kept the safety chain latched and opened the door. Tony Lee was sitting on the ground, one arm clutching an old-fashioned black doctor's satchel to his chest and the other tapping at my door. His eyes looked up at me, but I'm not sure they saw me. They were glassy and didn't focus. I pushed the door shut and undid the chain. I pulled the door open quickly and he fell to the floor, his front half sprawled over my threshold.

Worried about the neighbors calling the police, I grabbed him roughly by the collar of his jacket and dragged him the rest of the way into my small apartment, then shut the door and bolted it. He moaned quietly on the floor, but kept the bag close to him. For the first time, I noticed the satchel had the Infinity Corp logo embossed on the side. It was a Collector's kit, but a style we hadn't used in a few years.

"Rocket," Tony said quietly. "I got it, but…"

His voice trailed off and his head fell to the floor. I crouched next to him and checked the pulse on his neck. It was there, but weak. I gently took the satchel from him and set it to the side. The backside of the bag was wet and once out of the way, I could see why. Half of Tony Lee's torso was covered in sticky, dark blood. It had soaked through his jacket and attempting to peel that back only revealed his shirt, shredded, and his chest in a similar condition. There wasn't any spurting as if an artery had been nicked, but his skin had a sickly white tinge and he had lost a lot of blood. I knew the current lack of bleeding could be because his pressure was already far too low for him to survive.

I grabbed a couple of cushions from my couch and placed one under his feet; gently lifting his head, I rested it on the other. He was breathing, but just barely. I went quickly to my bathroom and grabbed my first aid kit. I kept more emergency supplies on hand than the average home-owner, but I couldn't compete with a hospital and that is where Tony needed to be.

When I returned to Tony his eyes had fluttered open and he was trying to say something.

"Hang on, Tony," I said as I pulled his shirt open.

The left side of his chest and stomach were shredded. It looked like a steak after a chef on meth had gone at it with one of those meat tenderizers. I applied a few clean bandages to cover as much of the open wounds as I could and wrapped it with stretch gauze, carefully feeding it under his prone body. It took me a moment to catch what he was mumbling.

"What did you say, Tony?" I asked. "What about Jack?"

"Jack found him…" he said quietly, his breathing ragged. Little bits of red froth bubbled from his lips when he spoke. I knew that was bad. He had blood in his lungs. He wasn't going to make it.

"Jack found who?"

"I didn't know. I just thought it was money." Tony's eyes were now closed more than they were open. I felt for a pulse again. It was sporadic and very weak. "Didn't think…"

His words drifted away just as his life did. I couldn't find a pulse. I checked the carotid and brachial. He wasn't breathing. He was gone.

I knew I needed to call the police. I couldn't hide his body and I didn't want to, but it was going to raise more questions than I had answers to give. I needed time. I checked his pockets for anything that might help, but there was nothing. His wallet had just a few dollars and plastic cards that seemed so meaningful when you were alive, but were as useful as a rainbow to a blind man after death. A photograph of a young Chinese girl that appeared to have been taken long ago. A sister maybe, or long lost love? I would probably never know.

I looked again at his bloody torso. I had managed to bandage the majority of the damage, but it was too severe to be covered by my simple medical kit. Looking around the edges of the most concentrated area of damage I could now make out dozens of tiny pinprick-sized holes. Tony Lee had been blasted by a needle gun. That explained the damage and the blood in the lungs. There was nothing that could have been done for him. His insides probably looked even worse than his outsides, and considering he looked like he'd been sent through a trash compactor, that was saying something.

One will get you a hundred that it was the same needle gun that had done in Stanley Morris and Ryan Middleton in the alley. Whoever had killed Tony was up to three murders, and if you took Jack Bowman into consideration there was a good chance it was four. At this point I could only think of two suspects: The mysterious Dawson Tillet— thought by most to be dead—or whoever Tillet was running from. Either way, I was worried I was on the hit list. I'd be damned if I was getting killed over something I still didn't even understand.

The black satchel with the Infinity logo sat off to one side where I had placed it. I slid it over and opened it. This particular style had already been out of use when I'd started with the company, but Collectors before me had carried them. The newer cases had more security as the company's legal division had realized one day that we were walking around with twenty-five million dollars' worth of equipment with us. My case required a fingerprint scan plus a twelve-digit code that had to be changed every thirty days. Fortunately for me, this case required only a simple clasp to be undone.

The interior of the satchel was a mess and smelled like a butcher shop when I opened it. At first I thought the smell of blood was coming from Tony, but this wasn't the coppery aroma of fresh blood; this was older, starting to go rotten. If the bag didn't already have maggots inside, it would soon. There was nothing I wanted less in this world at that particular moment than to put my hand inside, but Tony had clearly died for whatever it contained.

I opened the bag as far as it would go and tried to get as much overhead light into its interior as I could. A few of the collection tools—last generation, same as the satchel—were still in their appropriate spots, but many others were tossed about inside and tacky with half-dried blood. At first I tried to be as careful as possible—several of the instruments were razor sharp and I had no desire to contaminate myself with whoever's blood was inside—but then I realized there was an easier way.

I flipped the bag upside down and dumped the contents on my floor next to Tony's body. I decided it wasn't going to make my living room floor look any more like a murder scene. I nudged the tools around, trying to see find what was so important. It only took a second for me to spot it: A small black cylinder of textured metal. It was roughly the size of a can of soda and hinged on the long side so that it opened like a clam. I hadn't used this particular model, but I was familiar with it.

A splatter of dark blood had covered the LED on the top, but I scraped it away with my thumbnail to find a blinking blue light. There was an Infinity Corp memory implant inside and it was attached to the temporary power supply of the transport unit. A small recessed black button sat under the light. I pushed it and the container opened with a quiet click.

Inside a piece of square ceramic about the size of a postage stamp was embedded into a mesh of complicated electronics. The sideways "8" logo of Infinity Corp was printed in the center and a six-digit serial code was listed underneath. Somehow Tony had found the missing implant. I now knew that it wasn't the implant of Dawson Tillet, but rather Ryan Middleton. Who he was, I had no idea. The only way I could find out was to go back into the office.

Between Tony's death and the discovery of the missing memory implant, I found myself with a renewed sense of energy and purpose. I still didn't know what was going on exactly, but I was getting closer and now I had a bargaining chip. In addition to possessing the missing memory implant, I thought I was the only one who knew that Dawson Tillet wasn't actually dead, or at the very least wasn't the body in the alley. That was also valuable to the right people, particularly Tillet.

Before I left my apartment I called Detective Thorsen. When he answered he sounded groggy, but became alert as soon as I started speaking.

"Thorsen, it's Malone."

"What is it?" To his credit, he didn't comment on the obscene hour. He knew I wouldn't have called at 5 a.m. without a damn good reason. "You have it?"

"Tony Lee is dead. He's in my apartment, but I didn't do it. He showed up at my doorstep bleeding and I couldn't save him. I know you have questions and I don't have many answers, but I'm trying to get some. Give me a bit of a head start and I promise I will do what I can to help you with your investigation."

"You know I can't promise that," Thorsen said.

"I know you can't," I said. "But I also know you will."

I gave him the address and hung up before he could ask anything else. They would look for me at the office as well so I had to act fast. I grabbed the keys to my rental and left the building.

Chapter 20

"GETTING A BIT OF an early start, sir?" the guard at the front desk asked as I badged my way into Infinity Corp headquarters at 5:30 a.m. There was no one around apart from the cleaning crew and the guard.

"I've been keeping a lot of strange hours recently, it seems," I said.

Unfortunately I didn't have any idea how to use the Verification equipment and the security protocols in place wouldn't have allowed it even if I did. I couldn't jack the memory implant into the system and learn anything about it that way. What I could do was check the serial number stamped into the surface. There was only one problem— our client list was kept confidential, even from us. I could enter the six-digit code into the database, but once I did it would trigger a series of events.

The client's information would be revealed to me, but Infinity's system would now show that he was deceased and move on with the appropriate next steps. Of course, there were ways for some employees to avoid this, but as a Collector my job was only to deal with the clients after they had died. If I needed the info, the system assumed the person I was looking up was dead. If the memory implant that Tony Lee had brought me did in fact belong to the severed head of Ryan Middleton, then in theory it wasn't that big a deal. Middleton was clearly dead; even my limited medical training could have deduced that. But once I started the cogs of the Infinity Corp machine moving, it would be much tougher for me to act without attention from my employer.

I had to risk it, though. Tony had died delivering this implant and I had to know why. I pulled up the client database system and entered the six-digit serial number from the ceramic chip. The system then asked for the reason for my query. I clicked on Collection and entered my password. It took the high-powered network only a moment to pull up the file.

A biographical page appeared on my screen. A pop-up window warned that I had now indicated the client as deceased and proceeded with collection. Verification, Activation, and Legal had all been notified. As I read, I knew alerts were being sent out to the various on-call staff from those departments.

A photograph of Ryan Middleton was displayed in the upper left portion of my screen. He was a good-looking, middle-aged white guy. The photo appeared to have been taken on a boat and a beautiful, much younger woman stood at his side. He was fifty-seven years old and married. He had two children. He lived, or at least had lived, in New York City and was the owner of a financial management firm. So far nothing stuck out as particularly strange. He appeared to fit the demographic of eighty percent of our clientele.

For Tony to take off and leave me in the dark, either he must have learned something from Stanley Morris's memories, or Jack Bowman must have told him something on the phone. It was probably a bit of both. But what could it have been? The data I could access for Ryan Middleton was pretty scarce. The file was restricted so that different departments could only access information important to their duties. For those of us in Collection, that wasn't much. All we were really required to do was check the photograph and physical description against the body we pulled the implant from. It was just a simple cross-check to make sure there weren't any screw-ups.

I remembered the folded-up printout of Stanley Morris's recorded image. It was the grainy image of a man pointing a gun at him. It was dark and the face wasn't perfectly clear, but as I held it up to the screen it was definitely not Ryan Middleton. Middleton had gray hair and a thin build. The figure in the image was dark-haired and had an athletic, more muscular frame. It must have been Dawson Tillet.

Tillet must have killed both Ryan Middleton and Stanley Morris, but why? And why chop off the head of Middleton and take it with him? I thought about the Interpol flyer that Mr. China had shown me on Selene Belle. Fraud. Extortion. Embezzlement. Were Selene Belle and Dawson Tillet involved in some sort of scam of Ryan Middleton? The guy was clearly loaded, like all of Infinity's clients. If so, how did Stanley Morris fit into the equation? Thomas Arthur claimed Morris was one of his digital spies. So was Tillet, supposedly. It felt like a double-cross had gone down, but I didn't know why or how.

I had too many questions and not enough answers. The Verification staff member on call would be arriving soon, summoned by the alert I'd triggered. I didn't want to answer the questions that would surely arise when they got here, so I needed to go. The power supply in the portable collection case would keep whatever data was still in the implant safe for at least a few more hours, so I decided to take it with me.

As I returned downstairs to the main lobby, I saw someone from Verification badging herself in. Cindy something or other? I couldn't remember, but I knew she was one of Tony's colleagues. I ducked into an alcove behind a large plant and waited for her to get into the elevator. When she got upstairs and saw there was no implant for her to process, she'd start making calls. I was running out of time. To top it off, the police were certainly at my apartment by now and had found the body of Tony Lee. They would be coming to Infinity to look for me. Soon they'd be scouring the entire city trying to find me.

I gave the guard a curt nod as I exited and found my rental car parked out front. I needed to find Selene Belle and some answers.

Chapter 21

A FEW HOTEL GUESTS WERE up and about by the time I arrived at the Willard. Most were on their way to the restaurant to partake of the magnificent buffet breakfast. The smell of eggs cooking and high-quality coffee almost caused me to detour. At this point, I thought it might be worth getting arrested if I could get a good meal in first. I realized how little I had eaten in the last day or two. Cigars and police station instant coffee did not a healthy lifestyle make. Then again, neither did twenty to life for murder, so I decided to press on.

I asked the front desk agent at the hotel to call Selene Belle's room. As she pulled it up in the computer and started to dial, I made a mental note of the number. It almost certainly corresponded to the room number. I put my hand down on the receiver to cut it off before the call could go through.

The woman behind the desk blinked and almost lost her high-end-hotel smile of servitude.

"I'm sorry about that," I said. "I just suddenly realized how early it is, and I'd hate to wake my friend. Perhaps I'll just have breakfast first and then have you call."

"It is quite alright, sir," the woman said, the smile sliding back into place. "We have a wonderful buffet just across the lobby."

I thanked her and headed that way. Before I made it to the restaurant I looked back and saw that she was on to the next customer, a family with small children that appeared to be checking out. I slid off to the side and went to the elevator bank, taking the lift to Selene Belle's floor.

It was quiet, and most of the rooms—Selene's included—had 'Do Not Disturb' signs hanging from the door handles. I pressed my ear against the door and listened, but I couldn't hear anything inside. I hoped she was just sleeping and hadn't slipped out of town without telling me. Selene struck me as someone that had mastered the art of a quick getaway, particularly when the situation got hot.

I rapped lightly on the door with the back of my knuckles and listened again. I could hear movement in the room. It was a few seconds before footsteps approached the door and I heard Selene's voice from the other side.

"Who is it?" she said, her voice deep from sleep.

"It's Malone," I said. "We need to talk."

She opened the door a crack and confirmed it was me. She got on her tiptoes, trying to see behind me as though I had brought all of Interpol down on her. Her room was dim behind her, only a bedside lamp turned on.

"I'm alone. Just let me in."

She closed the door and undid the safety latch. I entered and shut the door behind me, locking the deadbolt and the safety latch. If she was nervous about this, she did a good job hiding it. Selene wore a silky nightgown of dark red that fell to just above the knee and clung to her curves like a high-end sports car. The front was low-cut and she stood boldly, with no concern for covering herself. For a moment I forgot why I had come to see her, but I made myself focus. I'd dealt with her type before. She had her weapons on full display, no different than a punk on the street corner who wanted you to see the piece tucked in the back of his pants.

"What is it, Mr. Malone? Have you found Dawson? His... head, I mean?"

I walked past her into the bedroom and did a quick survey. Her suitcase stood in the corner, already mostly packed. She was ready for a quick escape if necessary. I didn't see any signs that anyone else had been in the room. She followed me in and sat down on the edge of the bed. I took a seat at the nearby desk, not wanting the extra distraction of sitting too close to her. I could smell the lavender from her shampoo when I walked by.

"Tell me about Stanley Morris."

"Stanley Morris?" she said. "Why are you asking about him?"

"So you know who he is?"

"I... do, but what does it matter?" she asked. She turned to face me more straight on, sliding one leg casually over the other. "Why don't you come sit over here, Mr. Malone? It is too early to be holding a conversation across the room like this."

"I think we're fine right where we are. Now, you were about to tell me about Stanley Morris. What was he doing in that alley with Dawson Tillet? You said Tillet was undercover. Meeting him. What does that mean?"

"He was nobody, Mr. Malone. Just a..." She looked to the floor, trying to find the right word, but I already knew it.

"A mark?"

Selene jerked her eyes to mine, searching my face for a clue as to how much I already knew. "Whatever Mr. China has told you—"

"Isn't the half of it, I'm sure. I'm no angel myself, Miss Belle, but I need to know what I'm dealing with. You and Dawson Tillet were scamming Stanley Morris. Is that right?"

She bit at her lower lip and nodded. "Yes, that's correct." She stood and came and sat on the corner of the bed closest to me, her hand reaching out to touch my knee causing her to bend forward, her slip hanging down. "But nobody was supposed to get hurt. Nobody was supposed to be killed. I swear it, Mr. Malone."

"Did you know that Morris was one of Thomas Arthur's spies?" I asked.

She pulled her hand back quickly and raised it to her chest as though I had slapped her. "You know about that?"

"Sure I do," I said. "Thomas Arthur told me about it. Unless I'm mistaken, he's your employer."

Fire flashed in her eyes. "He is not my employer. He just... hired me to do something for him."

"I think that is what 'employer' means. And let me guess: you decided to handle things a bit differently? To not do what you were hired to do?"

She didn't answer, picked absently at a nonexistent thread on her nightgown.

"You're not safe, Selene. He knows you've betrayed him."

She nodded, but didn't say anything.

"And he knows you're here."

"In Washington?" she asked, her eyes wide.

"In the Willard Hotel."

She gasped and looked around the room, mentally packing her things, ready to run. "But how can he know that?"

I gave a little tilt of my head and a smile. I saw the realization hit her like a smack to the forehead.

"Mr. China," she said. "That little weasel. He went to Arthur, didn't he? I should have left him to rot back in France."

"I have to say, you don't surround yourself with the best company."

"Present company excluded?" she asked, her hand returning to my knee.

"I'm afraid you just don't know me very well."

She leaned in, her face just inches away, the front of her nightgown plunging and leaving what little was left to the imagination on full display. I could feel her warm breath on my lips and pick out the tiny specks of gray in her otherwise dark brown eyes.

"Perhaps I'd like to get to know you better," she whispered. "Rocket."

I pulled her close to me and felt the softness of her lips, the heat of her body mixing with my own. Selene Belle was a con artist, a grifter. Her power was in her beauty, her seduction, and the ability to adjust her strategy at the drop of a hat. She had just decided that I was the best course of action now.

I knew all of this as we sank into that kiss, my hands combing through her dark hair before moving on to explore her body. I knew she was using every tool in her kit to bring the situation back under her control.

That didn't mean I didn't enjoy the moment.

Chapter 22

As we pulled up in front of the army surplus store, I could see the doubt on Selene Belle's face. Even at this early hour, there were several less-than-savory-looking individuals hanging out on the corner nearby. Graffiti tags covered most of the flat surfaces and two kids sat on a stoop throwing rocks at any pigeons who got too close.

"Are you sure we can trust this guy, Rocket?" Selene asked for the third time since I told her my plan.

"He might be a crook," I said as we got out of the car, "but Attila does have a code. If he agrees to watch over you, there is nowhere in the city you'll be safer. Thomas Arthur will never be able to get to you here."

I hit the buzzer on the front door. The shop was closed, but I knew someone was always around, seeing as it doubled as Attila's home and base of operations. I was surprised to see Stevie let us in. I didn't think she lived here, and the store didn't open for a few more hours.

"A bit early for you, eh, Stevie?" I asked as she eyed Selene Belle.

"I could say the same for you, Rocket. Who's she?" Selene had her long coat pulled tight around her, but even with that bit of discretion she stood out in this shop like a Tiffany engagement ring in a church rummage sale.

"A friend. Is the Hun around? I need to speak with him."

She hit a buzzer under the counter and waited, her chin resting on her hands, making no effort to hide the fact she was staring at Selene.

"You ever think about getting your septum pierced?" Stevie asked Selene. "I think it would look real nice on you. You've got the right cheek bones."

Selene smiled weakly, taking in the dozens of visible piercings on Stevie. "No, I don't think it's for me," she said quietly. "It looks very nice on you, though."

Stevie nodded, her long earlobes dangling and clattering like wind chimes. The door in the corner clicked and Ladykiller Lou came out, looking energized and ready to face the day, even at this early hour.

"Rocket," he said, a big smile splitting his little rat face. "How wonderful to see you. And who is this ravishing creature?"

Lou slid over to Selene and draped an arm over her shoulders, the top of his head barely reaching her shoulder, but putting his face uncomfortably close to her breasts. "My name is Lou and it's my pleasure to make your acquaintance, Miss...?"

Selene sidestepped to escape his arm and offered her hand. "Selene Belle. I am a friend of Mr. Malone's."

Lou took her hand and kissed it on the knuckles, his other hand brushing lightly along her forearm. "It is a pleasure to meet you, Miss Selene Belle. I will not hold your choice of companions against you. We all make mistakes."

"Yeah, that's enough, Ladykiller," I said, stepping in and removing her arm from his grasp. "She is here to see Attila, not be groped by your little monkey paws."

Lou looked at Selene and sighed as though to say, "You see what I mean?"

"Fine. I am sure we will have a chance to become better acquainted later." Lou winked at Selene and she grimaced. He didn't appear to notice.

We followed him to through the door and past the gun room. Selene took it all in, her eyes wide, but she didn't say anything. At the second door we were buzzed in by Sergei and entered the elevator down to Attila's personal quarters. Whether Sergei even noticed Selene, or me for that matter, was tough to tell. He made no indication that he knew we were there. I was starting to wonder if Sergei hadn't grown up a bit too close to Chernobyl.

As we walked, Lou talked nonstop, mostly to Sergei, occasionally to us, but no one replied apart from the odd grunt from his Russian friend. I wasn't sure where he found time to breathe as he recapped television shows, stories he had heard, girls he had seen walk by, and every other inane detail of his life.

Selene whispered to me, "Why do they call him 'Ladykiller'? Is it some sort of joke? I can't imagine any woman ever being interested in that."

"Sort of a joke, but a bad one. It's quite a literal nickname. When Lou was just a kid he had a crush on this girl in his class. He was obsessed. Pretty much the same as this." I waved my hands at Lou and his continuing stream of chatter. "Of course she rejected him. In front of most of the school."

"And he killed her?" Selene asked, her hand to her face.

"They never proved it was him, but her parents found her the next day in the backyard, a bloody shovel next to what was left of her face."

"That's awful," Selene said.

"No argument here," I said. "Don't worry about him, though. If Attila says he'll take care of you, Lou won't bother you. He knows better than that."

We reached Attila's room, and he sat at a table in the corner eating a breakfast of steak and eggs. He looked up as we entered, but didn't rise.

"Malone," he said around a mouthful of eggs. "I didn't expect you back so soon. And I see you've brought a friend."

"Attila," I said as we approached. "This is Selene Belle."

She reached out a hand, and he wiped his off on a napkin and shook it. "Hello, Miss Belle." He went back to eating, but spoke to me. "She's very beautiful, Malone, but I don't take in women for debts. Not anymore."

"What does he—?" Selene started turning to me with panic in her face.

"She's not to pay off my debt," I said, placing my hand on her arm in an attempt to calm her down. "She needs help and I can't think of anyone better suited than you."

"I don't take in charity cases, Malone."

"He does," I said to Selene.

"I don't," Attila repeated, stuffing a bit of steak into his mouth. "I'm a businessman."

"Besides, I'm not talking about a charity case. I'm talking about a business deal. Selene is about to come into a considerable sum of money. However, there are certain individuals out there who are trying to stop that. If you can just keep her safe for a few days, we will pay you twenty thousand dollars. That will also cover my debt, of course."

Attila continued chewing loudly, never taking his eyes off his scrambled eggs. He was interested. Selene looked over at me nervously. I hadn't told her anything about any money or my debts, but she was smart enough to stay quiet. I knew she was afraid of Thomas Arthur and feared what he would do.

At last Attila cleaned his plate, picked up his napkin and dabbed at his face. He crumpled it up and dropped it on the plate and pushed back from the table. We followed him as he went to his leather recliner near the fireplace and sat.

"How long?" he asked at last.

"Two, maybe three days," I said. "Long enough for me to take care of the problem."

"Take care of the problem? Not exactly your style, Steven."

"Not that way," I said. "The guy I'm dealing with doesn't want Selene. Not when it comes down to it. He wants his property. I'm going to get it for him and convince him to move on. It's business to him. You understand."

Attila nodded. "I do. Twenty-five thousand."

It wasn't a question. I'd known he would raise the stakes. If Thomas Arthur came through and paid me the hundred grand for the memory implant, another five thousand wouldn't make a difference.

"Fine," I said. "You'll see to it that Lou keeps his paws off her?" I could see Ladykiller Lou and Sergei in the far corner shooting pool. They didn't pay any attention to us. They knew to stay out of the boss's business without an invitation.

"Lou won't trouble her," Attila said. He looked to Selene. "You don't have to worry about nothing when you're in my house. I've got a room you can have to yourself. You need anything, you just come to me."

"Thanks, Attila," I said. "I just need to talk to Selene and then I'll get out of your hair."

He waved at the air, unconcerned about what I did. I grabbed her by the elbow and led her to a quiet corner.

"I don't know, Rocket," she said as soon as we were out of earshot. "I don't know this man and this entire place, it's... well, it's just bizarre. And I don't have twenty-five thousand dollars to pay him with."

I shushed her. "Don't you worry. I'm going to deal with Thomas Arthur. Too many people are ending up dead and I think you're high on the list."

She nodded, tears filling her dark eyes. "It was supposed to be so easy. Dawson promised me that nothing could go wrong."

"You had to know it would go wrong someday. I've seen the rap sheet, Selene."

"But it's not true, Rocket," she said, raising her voice for a moment before bringing it down again. "Well, most of it isn't. Some of those things... I mean, I was there, but I didn't—"

"I'm not here to judge. I've got a past as well. I'm focused on the present. Leave everything to me. If all goes well, I'll have Thomas Arthur out of your hair, out of both of our hair, by the end of the day. Tomorrow at the latest."

She wrapped her arms around me and pulled me tight. Her lips brushed against my cheek. "Thank you, Rocket."

If she knew half of what I was keeping from her, she might have sung a different tune, but that was the game. She had her secrets, and I had mine. I just hoped they didn't burn us both in the end.

Chapter 23

I WALKED OUT OF ATTILA'S place to find the sun had finally risen on the lazy winter day. It was clear and cold, and the wind cut through my jacket like a shark through water. I turned my collar up in a futile attempt at warmth.

The drive back to the Watergate was quick. Traffic was still light, but it would be picking up soon. Washington, DC was notorious for its congestion and in an hour or so it would take forever to just a few blocks across the relatively small geography of the District. I parked in a guest spot and went in to the front desk. It was the same young man working as the first time I'd visited.

"Detective," he said. "It's good to see you again. Here to see Mr. Arthur?"

I took a quick glance at his name badge. "Jason, how have you been? Yes, I'll be seeing Mr. Arthur."

"And is he expecting you?" Jason scanned a list of guests, obviously not seeing my name.

"He should be. It was a rather last-minute deal, though, so I may not be on there." Before he could speak, I cut him off. "Jason, tell me. Have any other police been by? This morning or during the night?"

"No, sir," he said as we walked toward Arthur's apartment. "Not that I am aware of, though I did just come on shift." He rang the bell for the residence and turned to leave. "It was good to see you again, Detective."

The door opened and Walter stood there, his nose still swollen and his eyes purple from my handiwork. If I was honest, my own jaw could have looked a bit better as well. We stood eyeing each other for a moment, each waiting for the other to make a move. Finally, he turned and walked back inside without saying anything—my invitation to enter, I assumed.

I found Thomas Arthur in the living room, reading a book and admiring the view over the Potomac River. He set the book down as I arrived and stood to greet me.

"Mr. Malone," he said, shaking my hand. "Such an early visit. I do hope it means you have brought me good news."

I looked around the room, but apart from Walter standing at attention nearby, it didn't appear that anyone else was home. Arthur noticed my surveillance.

"If you're looking for Mr. China, I'm afraid he is not here. I am a good host, but I'm afraid that extends only so far. I assume he is back at his hotel."

"And what about Selene Belle?" I asked.

He laughed. "Why, you are a clever one, aren't you? No, I'm afraid I have not seen Miss Belle in some time. It would seem that she has decided to leave my employ."

"I didn't realize that was an option."

"Well, Mr. Malone. It is always an option. I am not a monster. Of course, I do reserve the right to recall my people and I expect them to answer. It is only reasonable."

We took a seat in the living room, a glass coffee table between us.

"I've come to make a deal, Mr. Arthur," I said. I pulled out the small black cylinder containing the memory implant of Ryan Middleton and set it on the table between us.

Thomas Arthur's eyes widened and a smile spread across his face. "So you have it, then. You have found it. To be honest, I was not too confident that you could do it."

"Not exactly," I said. His face fell, all of the mirth slipping away. "This isn't Dawson Tillet."

"That was not the arrangement, Mr. Malone."

"There's been a change in plans. I'm proposing a new deal."

"I am listening," he said.

"This is the memory implant of a man named Ryan Middleton. He was the owner of a small private investment firm in New York City. With his memories you would have the access to dozens if not hundreds of bank accounts of very wealthy individuals. Who knows what else he might know?"

Thomas Arthur licked at his lips. I knew appealing to his greed would get his attention, but the promise of further secrets was the real bait. "And how did you come to have this? Certainly your employer will discover you took it."

"Nobody knows I have it. No one will know that you have it. It was an off-the-books operation."

Arthur's eyes snapped from the container to me. I could see him trying to figure out what could have happened. Had I killed Ryan Middleton just to get the memory implant so that I could sell it? I would never have done such a thing, but perhaps he thought he had underestimated me.

"And this is to make up for the fact that you were unable to retrieve Dawson Tillet's memory implant for me?"

"A token of goodwill, not to mention I need the cash. Besides, whatever it is Dawson Tillet knows that you want so badly, it will be largely degraded by now. The police haven't found the head. No one has contacted Infinity Corp. It's probably rotting in some schizophrenic homeless guy's hovel and all of the precious contents inside along with it."

I knew this was important to Arthur. It had never been solely about retrieving the memories of Dawson Tillet for him. It had also been about keeping them out of the hands of his enemies. Tillet knew too much about Arthur's operation. I knew a little, what he had revealed, but I didn't know the inner workings like Tillet must. If Thomas Arthur thought that Tillet was dead and never to be worried about, he might just let it go. My offering of Middleton was just a bit of extra icing on the cake.

"A hundred thousand dollars," Arthur said. "The same offer as before?"

"And forget about Selene Belle," I said. "She's not one of yours anymore."

The smile returned to Arthur's face. "Ah, now I see. You do understand that is what she does, Mr. Malone? She seduces to get what she wants. She uses her beauty, her charm. She is using you."

"Take it or leave it, Arthur," I said, unwilling to address what I knew full well to be true. "You won't go after Selene. She's got enough problems without you adding to them."

"I'm not sure I can do that. You see, it sets a bad precedent. I hired her to seduce Stanley Morris, but she decided to go into business on her own. When a better offer came along, she took it. How can I not punish such disobedience?"

"And then she hired Mr. China?" I asked, putting the pieces together.

"And then promptly left him in police custody in France once she had gotten what she needed. You see, she has a bit of a bad habit of using men and leaving them chewed up and spat out behind her. You really do not want to be involved with her."

It made sense. It was what I'd always suspected about Selene. She was a seductress. Despite what most might think, it wasn't her body that was her greatest weapon; it was her mind. She used what she had to fool all of the men around her. Now she was probably doing it to me, but a deal was a deal.

"I know the risks," I said. "One hundred thousand dollars, in cash, and you leave Selene Belle alone. I so much as smell Walter in the area, and I'll return him to you in a box. A small one."

The young gun man glared over at me, but didn't leave his post. I'd have loved for him to try and take another shot at me when I was expecting it. The kid needed to learn some manners and I was just the teacher for the job.

"There is no need for such violence, Mr. Malone. Very well. It is a deal." He reached out his hand for me to shake. Right before I grasped it, I stopped.

"One more thing," I said.

"You are beginning to test my patience," Arthur said, the ever-present smile slipping. "What is it?"

"I'm not taking the rap for any of these murders. I didn't commit them and I'm not having you get out of town and leave me swinging from a rope. We need a fall guy. I vote for Walter."

This time the young tough did leave his post. He came charging toward me and I jumped to my feet, ready to receive him.

"Enough, Walter!" Arthur shouted. "You will do as you are told. Back over there. There's a good lad."

Thomas Arthur turned to me after calming the young man, though I could still hear Walter breathing hard. "You really shouldn't antagonize him so. But I see your point."

"Mr. Arthur, I—" Walter started, but at a look from Arthur, he slammed his mouth shut so hard I heard his teeth come together.

"I will not leave Walter to hang. He is like family to me."

I could tell the rich man wasn't going to budge on this. I didn't know what his connection to the kid was, but it was strong. "Fine. Mr. China. A strange foreigner in town, packing heat. The cops won't ask too many questions if we line him up just right."

Arthur nodded. "Yes, I suppose they won't. Fine."

"I'm going to need more than that. I need something to feed the police."

"Leave that to me, Mr. Malone. As I've told you many times before, I have many people in my employ. Several work for the police in the highest ranks. You lead them to Mr. China, and I will ensure that no one asks too many questions about the how and the why. Let them have their who."

Thomas Arthur stood and left the room. Walter kept his post, but stared daggers at me, waiting for me to say something. He wanted an excuse to draw and gun me down. I was too close, though. My mouth had gotten me into plenty of trouble of the years, but when I was this close to a hundred grand, I could keep it under control.

After a few minutes, Arthur returned with a small brown briefcase and gave it to me. I looked inside and saw multiple thick stacks of green bills. I didn't bother to count. Thomas Arthur might be a criminal, but shortchanging me on the deal wasn't in his nature.

Now I shook his hand. "It's been a pleasure doing business with you, Mr. Arthur." I started to leave, but turned back. "I do have one question."

"Yes, Mr. Malone?"

"Who was Stanley Morris? Why were you after him?"

Arthur chuckled. "Merely a loose end. It seems Mr. Morris had accrued a significant amount of debts to a local bookie. Because of his vices, he was being pulled into some moonlighting that I didn't approve of."

Now I understood Stanley Morris's final words about the Hun. He must have thought Attila had sent someone to settle the debt. I knew the feeling.

"One of your spies going rogue?"

"Let's just say he couldn't stay away from the race-track. You would have liked him." Arthur smirked at me knowingly.

"Somehow I doubt it." Fact was, Morris's fate easily could have been my own. It still might be if I didn't get some of this money to Attila.

"It has been an adventure, Mr. Malone." He walked me to the front door. When we got there he reached into a pocket and pulled out a business card. "If you should happen to come across the memory implant for Dawson Tillet, I am still in the market."

"Understood, but I don't think I'd worry too much about him. He's long gone."

As I walked down the well-manicured path leading away from his Watergate apartment, I heard him call out after me. "And Mr. Malone, don't forget what I told you about Selene Belle. It was beauty that slayed the beast."

Chapter 24

I SHOVED THE BRIEFCASE UNDER the driver's seat and sat for a few moments. My hands were shaking so I put them on the steering wheel. One hundred thousand dollars. I'd had that much in my hands in the past, but only fleetingly before I blew it all on the next 'sure thing.' There was so much I could do with the money. First, I knew I had to pay off Attila. It might take me a while to settle my debts, but I always did. Not to mention I'd more or less left Selene as collateral. I'm not sure she saw it that way, but I was certain Attila did.

Still, even after paying back Attila it left me seventy-five thousand dollars, less a few grand if I decided to toss a few bucks Selene's way. I should probably also help out with Jack's arrangements. I didn't know much about his family. A sister, I think? It was the right thing to do. And Tony Lee? Well, I had to draw the line somewhere. For all I knew, Tony had been working an angle of his own. It wasn't my fault he'd gotten shot before he could pull off whatever it was he meant to do. That's why he should have stayed in the lab and passed the call to me.

I found a nearby pay phone and stopped. I took the briefcase with me. The last thing I needed was some junkie stealing my car and my future along with it. If someone wanted this money, they were going to have to shoot me to get it. Even so, I'd do my damnedest to bleed on all of the cash as I was dying.

I pulled a card from my pocket and dialed. "Thorsen," the voice on the other end of the line answered.

"Detective Thorsen," I said. "It's Rocket Malone."

"Jesus, Malone," Thorsen immediately started, his voice as animated as I had ever heard in our short relationship. "What do you think you're doing? First your partner and now another co-worker, bled like a stuck pig in your living room. To top it off, he's got the same conspicuous wounds as two bodies found in an alley. You understand this doesn't look good, right?"

"Just take a breath, Thorsen. I've got your killer. Name's Mr. China. He's staying at the Willard Hotel, room 702."

"China?" he asked. I could hear him writing. "Got a first name?"

"As far as I know, he doesn't have one. Foreign guy. European."

"What makes you think he's the guy?"

"Let's just say he's been in the right place at all the wrong times."

"Malone, I'm going to need a heck of a lot more than that. If you've got—"

"Just run it up the food chain, Thorsen. I think you'll see it sticks."

There was silence on the other end of the line. I imagined the battle being waged in Detective Thorsen's mind. A hotshot young detective, new to the DC force. A series of high-profile killings and now a suspect delivered to him under dubious circumstances. Ethics were good, but sometimes putting on the right show was more beneficial.

"We'll get someone over there and see what shakes out."

"I thought you might," I said. "Between you and me, I don't think that missing head is ever going to turn up. The killer probably tossed it in the Potomac. It could be in the Atlantic by now."

"You mean Mr. China, right? The killer?"

"Yeah, I suppose I do. The way I figure it, he killed the two men in the alley. A professional hit. Who hired him? Beats me. Sees the guys had Infinity implants and decides to take the heads with him, but gets interrupted before he can get Stanley Morris. Goes after Tony Lee to cover his tracks."

"And Jack Bowman?" Thorsen asked, doubt in his voice. "How does he figure in?"

"Unconnected. Different murder weapon. Maybe Jack was just in the wrong place at the wrong time. Robbery gone bad. Jealous lover. Who knows?"

"Would you have bought this story when you were on the force, Rocket?"

I thought about it. I wanted to think I wouldn't. That my ethical standards wouldn't have allowed it. Then again, I'd taken bribes from drug dealers to turn a blind eye, so I was hardly a moral beacon.

"Yeah," I said at last. "If I was you, I would. This case isn't going anywhere, Thorsen. Just trust me. Take the gimme and go."

"I'm not sure I like how we police in DC," Thorsen said. "I thought it would be different here."

"It can be, but you need the power to make the changes. Get the power, Thorsen. Then make changes. It's all about the bigger picture."

"Was that your strategy?" Thorsen asked, no accusation in his voice. "Overlook the little things in hopes of a brighter future?"

"Maybe," I said. "I can't really remember any more."

For a moment neither of us said anything, both lost in our thoughts. Ghosts from the past for me and glimpses of the future for him. Detective Thorsen could make changes to the corruption and depravity of this city. I just hoped he lasted long enough to do it, before the Valentines, Attilas, and—if I was honest—Rocket Malones of the world pulled him down to our level.

"I'll be in touch, Rocket."

"I figured you would be. I've got a few affairs to take care of while you guys process my apartment. I'll give a full statement tomorrow. That work?"

"Yeah," he said. "I'll take care of it."

"Give my regards to Sergeant Valentine."

Chapter 25

THE SOUNDS OF AN EMPTY house comforted me. I didn't hear ghosts scuttling about or unseen terrors. Just life. The scratching of a bird's claws as it landed on the aluminum gutter above the window. A sudden pop in an unknown board as the wooden frame breathed in the changing temperature of the day. A loud truck driving by out front, causing just enough of a disturbance to finally force a dead branch on the maple in the backyard to bounce off of the roof. I could have sat and listened to it for days, just me and the solitude of a sleeping house.

It was the quick opening of a window from downstairs that roused me from my meditation. I had lost track of how long I'd sat in the upstairs bedroom, but the shadows had grown long across the hardwood floors. I might have been here for days, weeks without someone arriving, but I had a detective's hunch. Too many years of tracking down murderers had taught me to trust in these feelings that came from my gut, as it assembled the pieces of the puzzle far faster than my brain. This was why I sat for hours in a vacant house in the posh northwest neighborhood of Cathedral Heights.

I could hear him walking downstairs, not with the quiet steps of a burglar, but the confident stride of the master of the house. For the last few days, maybe even longer, that is what he had been. This was his house and he had used it as his base of operations, but there was a large duffel bag sitting in the room that told me he was ready to move on. It was zipped shut and stuffed with clothing. All I had to do was wait for him to come claim it.

The stairwell in the house was wood, but covered in an expensive runner of carpet. Everything about the house was nice and the place probably had a price tag that easily exceeded seven figures. Rising crime and dissatisfaction with the government were pushing out the rich, the white collar of Washington, DC. More and more houses like this sat empty, waiting for a buyer that might never come. Even with the fine wool carpet, I could hear him coming up the stairs. It was the steady, sure-footed climb of a man in his prime, a hunter.

At the top of the stairs he paused. Had the door to the bedroom been closed before? He would know it wasn't. He was a professional. He wouldn't have forgotten a detail like that. That is why he paused, knowing someone had been in the room—wondering if they still were. I stood quietly and listened as he played this drama out in his mind. After a moment the door to the bedroom flew open and he charged in. I could hear him, a slight explosion of breath as he readied himself to fight. But there was no one in the room. He would be doubting himself. Maybe it had blown shut from the wind? The house had been empty a long time apart from his temporary residence. Strange things happen to vacant houses.

It told me what I needed to know. He had seen a possible threat and charged forward to face it. He was wired for fight, not flight. I'd figured as much, but it was always good to verify. A good cop is a careful cop, and I was a good cop despite what anyone might have told you.

I stood in the corner of the bedroom, the open door blocking his sight of me until he stood nearly in the center, near his duffel bag. His peripheral vision caught me first and he turned to face me slowly. I must have startled him, standing there hidden in the shadow, but to his credit he hid it well. He was a professional and he had outplayed all of us for quite a while, but there was always someone better. This time it was me.

"Dawson Tillet," I said. "I've been looking forward to meeting you. Seems everyone's been looking for you lately. Part of you, at least."

He didn't say anything. I could see him calculating the distance and tensing his muscles for the short sprint. He was my height, but strongly built, not like a football player, more like a gymnast. I could hold my own, but I was smart enough to see a fight I didn't want to join. I closed the hinge of my elbow and brought my right hand up to waist level, the matte black of the gun pointed at his stomach.

"For a dead man you're looking quite well. Particularly healthy considering your head got chopped off."

"I've always had a strong constitution." His voice was deep, and with a bit of a southern twang I hadn't expected. Alabama, if I had to guess. "You must be Rocket Malone."

"I felt it was time we met in person. I cleaned up your mess for you."

He cocked his head to the side. "How's that?"

"Middleton, Morris…" I said. "Tony Lee?"

"That last guy got involved where he had no business. That wasn't personal."

"I'll be sure to pass that message along to his family. I'm sure they'll be happy to hear that." I didn't even know if Tony Lee had family, but Tillet's casual attitude toward death brought out my sarcastic side.

"So what do you want, Malone? If it's some kind of payout, you're barking up the wrong tree. You've been through the duffel. There's no cash in there. Just what little I got." He nodded toward the gun in my hand. "And it seems you've already helped yourself to the best of that."

"It's quite a piece," I said. "A flechette pistol. Needle gun. I've handled one a few times over the years, but in police work they pretty much discount them. No good in a firefight. Terrible accuracy. Almost no penetration. But I always thought in the right situation they were quite effective."

"That's right," Tillet said.

"Like when I'm standing ten feet away from you. I pretty much just need to hold the trigger down and watch you turn into a cloud of blood."

"But if you wanted to do that, you would have done it," he said. "So what is it you want? Not money. Not me."

"I want answers. I want to know why everyone has been so keen to get at that memory implant in your skull."

"I know things. Secrets that others don't want me sharing. I know all the ins and outs of Thomas Arthur's spy operation. The memories he's been harvesting. How his technology works. His contacts at Infinity Corp."

My face must have betrayed me. Dawson Tillet smiled a humorless grin. "You didn't think he had someone on the inside? You work for the company. You know how secretive they are about their technology. He didn't hack the system himself. He had someone help him. I know how it is. I know everything, Malone. I know too much. I realized one day that the only way I was getting out was dead."

"So that's what you did," I said. "The decapitation of Ryan Middleton wasn't to steal any secrets from his Infinity implant. It was to hide your tracks. Let everyone think it was you. But you had to know that wasn't going to last long. The police figured out the true identity of that body within a day."

"All I needed was a head start and the secrets in Middleton's implant would have financed a new beginning. Like I said, I know the Infinity contacts. They could have pulled all that banking information from Middleton's head for me. They would have, for the right cut."

"Then what happened? Why didn't you leave?"

My mind went back to that night. Jack and I back at Infinity Corp and the call from the guard downstairs. The first person that wanted to hire us for our services. "Selene Belle."

Tillet nodded. "Selene. Yeah. That's what she is going by these days. I didn't know she had followed me here. I damn well didn't expect she'd go try and hire you."

"But she did, and that messed up your plans. Was she in on it?"

"On what? Killing Middleton and Morris? She doesn't have the stomach for that sort of thing."

I wasn't so sure about that. I thought Selene would do whatever she needed to get what she wanted. Maybe she deluded herself about the devastation she sometimes left in her wake, but part of her knew. You can't go through life seducing and swindling marks without leaving some broken bodies behind. They were there whether you were around to see them or not.

"And Morris? He's another of Thomas Arthur's hired guns, right? Wasn't he just another guy doing a job?"

"Stanley Morris was an idiot. That's what made it all so easy. I told Morris I had a line on a new mark and that if he met him in the alley, I'd sneak in behind and take him out. I told him I'd bring him into my plan to get out from under Arthur's thumb. Morris was just stupid enough to believe it."

"So you took out both of them."

"Nope. There you're wrong. Stanley Morris killed Middleton for me. He panicked and starting shooting with that stupid needle gun of his."

Now it made sense. Something that had never quite clicked for me. "That's why you bought the book."

"I'm impressed, Malone. If the police still had you around they probably would've got me. Yeah, I knew Morris was jumpy and likely to start spraying the alley with flechettes."

"So you bought some instant armor. A book stuck in your shirt. It'd never stop a traditional bullet, but for a needle gun…"

"It was more than up to the job. After he killed Middleton I drew on him, but he must have figured out it was all a setup. He pulled the trigger first. You should have seen the stupid look on his face when he drained a few dozen of those needles into my chest without me batting an eye. I knocked that gun out of his hands and for good measure decided to give him a taste of it. Unfortunately for Morris, he was never much of a reader."

Dawson Tillet laughed at his own joke. During our back and forth he had managed to move a step or two closer to me. He was stupid if he thought I hadn't noticed, but it was dark in the room and he didn't have many options. He didn't know if I was going to take him, shoot him, or let him go. To be honest, I wasn't so sure myself.

"Arthur paid me for Middleton's implant. Tony Lee got it to me."

Tillet stopped laughing. His eyebrows pulled together and his lip curled. I guess he'd thought he still had that option open to him. The funding for his future life had just floated away, like the ashes from a dying fire.

"I should have used my own gun," Tillet said. "That needle gun is addictive, though, like something out of a video game. That nerd wouldn't have gotten away if I'd done him proper. He got a taxi and I couldn't follow."

"How'd he find you? Jack called him. He found you?"

"I don't know," Tillet said. The sun had dipped lower as we spoke and the room was growing dark. I could hardly make out the details of his face anymore. My arm was starting to cramp from holding the gun. "Your partner followed Selene here. He must have figured out something was up and decided to watch the house."

"She knew you were here? Selene?" I had suspected as much. She'd known the body wasn't Tillet's from the get-go. She'd wanted his disappearance to happen as much as he did.

"I called her that night. Before I knew she'd gone to you. I told her to come here."

"Because you're lovers. How do you know she isn't using you the same way she uses everyone else?"

Dawson Tillet laughed, but I didn't see how he could be so cocky. What made him think he couldn't be played by a beautiful woman? I was certain many of Selene's previous marks had felt the same way.

"Selene isn't my lover, Malone. She's my sister. She wouldn't ever betray me. We're twins."

It was hard to see him, but I felt stupid now for not having noticed. The picture of Dawson in the photograph from Stanley Morris's memories hadn't been great, but the features, the sharp cheekbones, the dark eyes. It was obvious now. The one person whom Selene wouldn't stab in the back. It was her brother. No wonder she had put herself at such risk, in the middle of Thomas Arthur's crosshairs.

"Jack knew something was up and called me, but got Tony. Why would Tony—?"

Before I could finish my thought out loud, Tillet made his move. He charged straight at me, his athletic build pushing him fast, hoping the element of surprise coupled with my weariness of holding the needle gun would give him a chance. I pulled down the trigger and heard the distinctive hiss of the compressed gas as it fired dozens, hundreds of short steel flechettes into the dark room. I could hear the sharp taps, like a rabid woodpecker attacking a tree, as the shards of metal flew into the wood walls around the room. I also hear the sudden intake of breath from Dawson Tillet as the needles stabbed into him, but then he was plowing into me.

A needle gun would completely shred any unprotected flesh at short range and the damage was nearly impossible to fix, regardless of medical care. The technology had a few major flaws, though. One, which Dawson Tillet had used to his advantage in the alley, was that any sort of protection was enough to stop the flechettes. Another disadvantage to the weapon was that it had very limited stopping power. The needles shot right through their target without slowing it down.

Dawson Tillet slammed me hard into the wall behind me and the gun fell to the floor. The room exploded momentarily into flashes of light when the back of my skull impacted the wood. In a moment we had collapsed to the floor, Tillet on top of me and using his superior strength to pin one of my arms to the hardwood while his other reached up for my throat. I reached out, trying to find the gun next to me, but also to keep from having the breath choked out of me.

My fingers landed on the cold metal of the gun's handle, but he grabbed my wrist and slammed it down hard on the wood, and pain shot up my forearm. Tillet's breath was ragged, and I could hear liquid gurgling in his mouth. Blood was in his lungs, the flechettes having torn him up in his desperate dash to get to me.

"Tillet," I said, my voice barking out through his attempts to get his fingers around my throat. "Give it up. You need a doctor."

"Too late for that," he said and we both knew he was right. "But I can take you with me."

In a final desperate lunge, he released my arm and shot the additional hand to my throat, managing to get both of his strong hands wrapped around my windpipe. He crushed down and almost instantly my vision started to narrow. It felt as though I was looking up at him through a long tunnel. Dawson Tillet would almost certainly die from his internal bleeding, but not before he strangled me to death. I scratched at his hands, but he was too strong. I couldn't break his grip.

I felt my thoughts growing foggy, my brain being denied oxygen. My hands slipped from his and onto my chest. There was something small and hard in my chest pocket. I pulled it out with my waning strength and used my thumb to flip open the cap. With my thumb I pushed down the button and ignited the jet of blue flame of the Ronson lighter. In the dark of the room, it shone like a star in the heavens. I shoved it up into his face, the flame sliding over his cheek and burning into his eye.

Dawson Tillet screamed, the fluid in his lungs turning the shout of pain into a gurgle. He instinctively pulled his hands to his seared eye, allowing the oxygen to return to my body. I hacked and coughed as I rolled away from him. Tillet fell backwards off of me. He tried to get to his feet, his hands still cupping his destroyed eye, but his strength was leaving him. He fell on his ass and pushed himself back so that he could lean against the wall.

I stood and grabbed the needle gun from the floor next to me. I pointed it at him, but saw that it wouldn't be necessary. Dawson Tillet was done for.

"It didn't have to go down this way," I said, my voice scratchy and raw.

He looked at me and for once I was glad for the darkness of the room. Even in the shadows I could tell that his eye was ruined. Blood bubbled from his lips. "Would you have let me go?"

"No," I admitted. "But prison would have beat this."

For a moment neither of us spoke; the only sound was Tillet's labored breathing.

"You know," Tillet said, "I didn't kill your partner."

I nodded, but he probably couldn't see it. "You and your sister were close?"

"Twins," he said. "Doesn't get much closer."

"I think this'll make a pretty good punishment."

He didn't respond. After a moment the room grew silent and I crouched down close, keeping the gun ready. Dawson Tillet didn't move, his one good eye staring straight ahead, seeing nothing. I reached down and grabbed one of his hands and turned it over. Even in the near darkness of the room, what little light there was gathered by the iridescent Infinity tattoo at the base of his wrist. Everything that had happened in the last few days was recorded in his brain.

It would have solved everything for the police. The murders in the alleyway. Jack Bowman. Tony Lee. Thomas Arthur's entire espionage operation. The problem was, it also would have ended with me killing him. Self-defense? The jury might see it that way. Or, they might see a disgraced cop who got a big payout to cover up a murder. I couldn't take the chance.

I walked over and grabbed my lighter from the floor where it had been dropped in the fight. I dropped the needle gun on Dawson Tillet's lap and then used my Ronson to light the edge of his shirt. I walked over to his duffel bag and looked around inside while his clothes started to smolder. He had a passport and a plane ticket to Mexico City. I ripped out the pages of the passport and tossed them on his lap along with the ticket, and they went up quick.

I stood to the side and watched for a few moments as the rest of his clothes caught fire and the flames started to crawl across the wall and the hardwood floor around him. I traced my steps back out of the house, wiping down the few places I had touched, got into my cheap rental car, and drove home.

Chapter 26

MY APARTMENT WAS A CRIME scene and I had the cash, so I decided it was time to splurge a bit. I rented a suite at the Willard Hotel. It quickly took a twelve-hundred-dollar chunk from my briefcase of cash, but I decided I had earned it. I noticed a few police standing around the lobby of the hotel and asked the woman at the front desk what was going on.

She leaned in with a conspiratorial whisper. "They came and arrested one of the guests." She looked around again to see if anyone was listening before adding, "For murder."

I thought of my new friend Mr. China. The guy creeped me out, and he had pulled a gun on me the first time we met, but I wondered if I hadn't done him wrong. Now that there was a body in a burned-out house in Cathedral Heights to take the blame, maybe I should give

Detective Thorsen a call. I decided to think on it and let China stew for a bit in jail.

The room was beautiful and I slept better than I had in months. When I woke I called in to the office and told my supervisor that I was too torn up over Jack and Tony to come in. They told me to take the time I needed. I decided a week would probably suffice.

Snow started to fall on the city, making even the wretched slum where Attila's army surplus store stood a winter wonderland—at least until the gray filth of the city overtook the beauty. I buzzed in and found Stevie reading a book behind the counter.

"What's the book of the day, Stevie?"

She held it up higher so I could see the cover, but didn't stop reading. It was *Snow Crash* by Stephenson. She hit a buzzer under the counter to call someone to the door. "Come back to pick up your girlfriend?"

"Something like that. Tell me something, Stevie. You got any brothers or sisters?"

She stuck her finger in her book and closed it to look at me. "A brother. Older. Why?"

"You close to him?"

She shrugged, a lock of raven-black hair streaked with deep purple falling into her eyes before she flipped it back behind her ear. "He's up in Baltimore. We talk every so often. Normal, I guess."

"If you did something really bad, what would you think if someone punished your brother for it?"

"I'd think that was a real shitty thing to do. He and I aren't the same person."

"What if he'd also done some really bad things?"

She thought for a moment. "I'd say it was still shitty, if he's getting extra grief thrown on him just because of something I did. Why are you asking, Rocket?"

"Curiosity."

The door to the back opened and Sergei loomed there. His little pig eyes glared at me through his beard and shaggy head of hair. Stevie gave him a little smile and went back to her book, her interest in my hypotheticals already gone.

Selene Belle ran up to me and wrapped me in her arms when I entered Attila's underground home. She had changed into a form-fitting red dress and carefully coordinated shoes. It was possible she had packed it, but I thought it shined of Attila's work. He would probably add it to the tab.

"Oh, Rocket," she said. I don't know when she decided to starting using my nickname, but I liked the sound of it coming from her. "I was frightened you wouldn't come back. Is everything taken care of with Thomas Arthur?" That sounded more like her true concern.

Attila walked up as we stood there. He brushed crumbs from the front of his shirt and finished chewing something. "You have my money, Steven?"

I detached myself from Selene's arms and turned to Attila. I reached into my jacket and pulled out two large stacks of bound hundred-dollar bills. I had only brought the money I owed Attila and left the rest in a safe-deposit box. Attila was an honorable sort as far as those things went, but an extra eighty thousand dollars right in front of him might cause him to remember a few other debts I had.

I handed the cash over. He flipped quickly through the stacks, taking in the numbers. I noticed Selene to the side with her hands to her mouth.

"Didn't think I could do it?" I asked her.

"I... well, of course I knew you could," she said, trying to recover her typical poise. "Does that mean you found Dawson Tillet's implant and gave it to Thomas Arthur?"

If Attila had any interest in what we spoke of, he did an excellent job of hiding it. Instead he focused on his cash.

"I made a different arrangement with Thomas Arthur," I said. "No one will ever get Dawson Tillet's memory implant."

Selene exhaled a held breath as relief visibly washed over her. "So he... his head, that is... has still not been found?"

Attila did raise an eyebrow at that and looked at me. I shook my head at him briefly. *You don't want to know*, it said. Attila was a savvy businessman. He knew when to get involved and when to stay out. This was a great case to stay as far away from as possible. He turned and walked over to his comfortable leather chair in front of the fire and took a seat. A plate of food sat next to him and he went back at it.

"No, it's been found." I watched her eyes. They widened a bit. "It was still attached to his body though. It was never Dawson Tillet in that alley."

"But I don't understand—"

"I think you understand just fine, Selene. You knew all along that your brother wasn't in that alley. It was all a hoax to throw Thomas Arthur off his trail."

"But how did you find out?" she asked, her hands made little fists at her side. "Where is my brother?"

I held for a beat and searched her face. Had she been playing me for a patsy from the very beginning? Had she ever felt anything for me, or was I just someone else to use and throw away, the same as she'd done with Stanley Morris, Mr. China, and who knew how many others?

"He's dead," I said at last.

She let out an involuntary whimper and brought her balled hands to her mouth. "You killed him?"

"He tried to kill me." I lifted my chin to show the scratches and bruising around my throat from Tillet's fingers. "In the struggle I shot him."

"You didn't have to—"

"What if I told you he admitted he killed my partner? He killed Jack Bowman?"

"But he…" She turned away suddenly and took a step. "He said that? He admitted to it, I mean?"

He hadn't, of course. He'd killed Tony Lee when he came around snooping the yard looking for Jack, but Dawson Tillet hadn't killed my partner. Someone else had lured Jack Bowman into the backyard of that house. If my partner had a weakness, it was a pretty face. He was a veteran, a fighter. He would have known better than to stumble blindly into the dark with a killer on the loose. He would only have gone if led by the right bait.

"Yeah," I said. "Your brother said he killed Jack. He was my partner. I couldn't let that go."

After a moment she turned back to me. There were tears in her eyes and one slipped free when she nodded vigorously toward me. "Yes, I can understand that. I never wanted my brother to come to this, but I can see you did what you had to do."

"I did what I had to do," I repeated. That was Selene Belle in one simple sentence. "And what about you? Where will you go now?"

"I don't know," she said. "I… I don't really have any money. I spent the last of what I had here in Washington. I don't suppose you could help me? Just for a little bit?" She stepped in closer to me and rested one delicate hand on my arm. "I promise I won't be any trouble. It is just until I figure out what is next for me."

I looked down into her beautiful, dark eyes, still moist from her tears. She had never looked more beautiful or more dangerous than she did at that moment. I reached into my jacket pocket and pulled out the last envelope I carried and gave it to her.

"What's this?" she asked, opening it to reveal the cash inside. "I don't understand…"

"Five thousand dollars. It's my gift to you. I want you to take it and I want you to get out of here. Away from Washington, DC, and away from me."

"Rocket, don't—" She tried to grab on to my arms, but I pulled her hands off of me roughly.

"I'd be quick about it if I were you. Thomas Arthur is still out there and he probably isn't happy with you. The way I hear it, Mr. China has a pretty legitimate beef as well. There's a train ticket in there for New York City. It leaves in an hour."

"But I thought we had something, Rocket. What about us?"

I turned and walked away, back to the elevator to return to the street. I didn't look back, but as I stood waiting for the door to open and take me away from Attila's, I spoke. "That was just a dream, Selene. For a moment I thought it was a good one, but now I'm wide awake."

Afterword

Thank you so much for reading. If you enjoyed the book, it would mean a great deal to me if you would consider doing two things.

1. Please take a few minutes to leave a review on Amazon. For indie authors like myself, reviews and word of mouth are crucial to our success. Your help goes a long way toward the future success of my books.

Please Leave a Review

2. Choosing to publish independently comes with many benefits, but there is no denying it is much tougher to get the word out. Because of that, I've started a mailing list for my readers. In addition to be the first to learn about new releases, I'll be doing giveaways of exclusive bonus material. And I promise, no spam.

Join the Newsletter: http://shawnkobb.com/newsletter/

About the Author

Shawn Kobb is an American author living in Vienna, Austria. In addition to writing mysteries and thrillers, he moonlights as a diplomat and has lived and worked in Ukraine, The Bahamas, Afghanistan, and Washington, DC. If he told you any more than that, he'd have to kill you.

Before joining the U.S. Foreign Service, he worked as a 911 dispatcher for a large city in the Pacific Northwest well-known for its rain. Not Seattle, the other one. While working as a dispatcher, he had ample opportunity to develop plot ideas while speaking on the phone with crime victims, murderers, naughty children, and schizophrenics.

He lives in Vienna with his wife, a dog, and a cat.

Also by Shawn Kobb

CITY OF GHOSTS
A MYSTERY IN VIENNA

Made in the USA
Charleston, SC
27 September 2015